"You Can't Hide in Forever, You Know."

Cassie heard J.K. continue to speak as he stood outside the door. "They want to lock up this place before morning. They'll throw you out eventually."

She marched out of the rest room, head held high. "What makes you think I was hiding out in there?"

J.K. grinned. "Experience."

"Maybe I was just trying to make myself more beautiful for you before we went home. Isn't that what all your dates do this time in the evening?" *Uh-oh,* Cassie thought. *Bad choice of words.* She saw J.K.'s whole body visibly tense at the flirtatious remark. "I mean, you go to your home and I go to mine. Not the two of us together."

She watched the flare of passion being rekindled in his eyes. "Oh, no! Forget it! You get that notion out of your head right this minute."

He nodded seriously, but there was the faintest suggestion of a smile playing about his lips. "Whatever you say, Cass. Whatever you say."

Dear Reader,

Welcome to Silhouette Desire! Naturally, I think you've made a spectacular choice because, for me, each and every Silhouette Desire novel is a delightful, romantic, unique book. And once you start reading your selection I *know* you'll agree!

Silhouette Desire is thrilling romance. Here you'll encounter the joys and even some of the tribulations of falling in love. You'll meet characters you'll get to know and like . . . and heroes you'll get to know and *love*. Sensuous, moving, compelling, these are all words you can use to describe Silhouette Desire. But remember, words are not enough—you must *read* and get the total experience!

And there is something wonderful in store for you this month: *Outlaw*, the first in Elizabeth Lowell's WESTERN LOVERS series. It tells the story of rough-and-tough Tennesee Blackthorne . . . a man of fiery passions and deep emotions.

Of course, *all* of February's Silhouette Desire books are terrific—don't miss a single one! Until next month . . .

All the best,

Lucia Macro
Senior Editor

SHERRYL WOODS

FEVER PITCH

SILHOUETTE *Desire*®

Published by Silhouette Books New York

America's Publisher of Contemporary Romance

SILHOUETTE BOOKS
300 East 42nd St., New York, N.Y. 10017

FEVER PITCH

ISBN: 0-373-05620-6

First Silhouette Books printing February 1991

Printed in the U.S.A.

SHERRYL WOODS

lives by the ocean, which, she says, provides daily inspiration for the romance in her soul. She further explains that her years as a television critic taught her about steamy plots and humor; her years as a travel editor took her to exotic locations; and her years as a crummy weekend tennis player taught her to stick with what she enjoyed most—writing. "What better way is there," Sherryl asks, "to combine all that experience than by creating romantic stories?"

One

"**I** am going to die!"

The dramatic declaration was accompanied by an exaggerated sigh. The teenager closed her eyes and clutched her still-flat chest with a swoon worthy of Scarlett O'Hara. She was propped upright by the two giggling girls on either side of her in the sun-drenched bleachers. Her eyes opened wide and she stared dreamily toward the dusty baseball field, where J.K. Starr was making his way toward the pitcher's mound.

"Did you see that, Heather? Did you? He winked at me. Midnight Starr actually winked at me. Did you ever see anyone that gorgeous in your entire life? Did you? I swear I am going to die."

J.K. listened to the breathless exchange and shook his head. He'd never gotten used to it, never understood why teenaged girls—or grown women, for that matter—carried on so just because he was wearing a baseball uniform. Not that he minded, but he was just an ordinary guy who'd grown up on a horse farm in Kentucky. He happened to throw a baseball with a fair amount of speed and accuracy. Women acted as if that made him some sort of sex god. His teammates never let him forget it, either.

As if on cue, Davey Ramon-Sanchez jogged up beside him and taunted, "Hey, amigo, you got another big fan over there. Why you not leave a few of the pretty ones for the rest of us?"

Davey, with his black curly hair and soulful brown eyes, had more than his share of adoring female followers. He also had a tiny spitfire of a wife who'd lynch him in center field if he even spoke to one of them. "You can have them all, my friend," J.K. offered generously. "Unless, of course, you're afraid of Maria."

Davey's grin faded and he quickly crossed himself while gazing devoutly heavenward. J.K. laughed at his comrade's instantaneous transformation into dutiful husband. "That's better, Sanchez. Now how about getting up to the plate and hitting the ball for a change, instead of letting me toss it past you?"

The third baseman rocked back on his heels and regarded him indignantly. "Tossing? What is this tossing? They clock you yesterday at ninety-seven miles an hour and that was after you slow down. No wonder the batters look like they sleep at the plate, Midnight Starr. They cannot even see your pitches."

J.K was more pleased by Davey's compliment on his pitching than he was by the adoration of his trio of pubescent fans. Being named the league's most valuable player for the past three seasons had been like a dream. Back in Kentucky, he'd grown up listening to Cincinnati Reds games on the radio long after his parents had insisted on lights-out. He'd idolized players like Johnny Bench and Pete Rose. He'd wanted nothing more than to grow up and play for the team they'd made great. Instead, he found himself playing against that team now and mourning Pete's downfall. Every time he struck out a Reds batter, he felt guilty. Well, a little guilty, anyway, especially if the score was already plenty lopsided.

"Hey, amigo," Davey shouted. "You going to throw the ball today or you taking the afternoon off?"

J.K. grinned. "You that anxious to make a fool of yourself, Sanchez? Let's see what you can do." Three straight fastballs over the inside corner left Davey standing flat-footed at the plate.

"Stop staring at the bleachers and keep your eyes on the ball," he advised the muttering batter. "Maybe I should throw it nice and slow, like I would for a girl. What do you think? I bet Maria could hit the ball better than you."

"You go to hell," Davey retorted, resuming his stance with a look of fierce concentration and slamming J.K.'s curveball into left field.

"I gave you one," J.K asserted, laughing. "Nice and easy, just like I promised."

"You gave me nothing," Davey said, clearly affronted by the charge. "Again, amigo."

Before J.K could complete his windup, though, manager Ken Hodges shouted at him from the dugout. "J.K., you got a phone call over here. The kid says it's important."

J.K jogged across the field, once again winking at the girls who were still gazing raptly from the sidelines. They erupted into another fit of high-pitched giggles as he stepped into the fancy dugout and reached for the phone. Ken held it just out of reach.

"Make it snappy," he warned. "You know how I feel about personal phone calls out here during practice. Besides, you ain't got no business giving this number to your fans."

"I don't give this number to my mother," J.K. swore, then snatched the phone from the still-grumbling manager. "Hello."

"Uncle Jake?"

J.K. recognized at once both the tentative little voice and the blending of his initials into one easy-to-say name. His heart seemed to go still. "Teddy? What's wrong?"

"You've got to come right away, Uncle Jake. It's an emergency. Mom..."

His heart revved up, pumping his blood harder and faster than any pitch he'd ever hurled. If anything had happened to Cassie...

Damn Ryan Miles for not being there.

J.K.'s best friend and former teammate had had the morals of an alley cat. He didn't have a lick of sense either, as far as J.K. could see. Only a fool would have walked off and left a terrific woman like Cassie to rear his son alone. J.K. had admitted to himself long ago that there was a soft place in his heart for Ryan's fragile, blue-eyed wife. She was a real sweetheart, gentle, good-natured and so pretty it had made him go breathless the first time he'd laid eyes on her. It had killed him watching the awful pain in her eyes when Ryan had told her lie after lie. She'd been a master of the brave front, though, pretending that she didn't recognize the evasions for what they were. He'd never met a woman he'd admired more or felt more inclined to protect from life's hard knocks. Unfortunately, he hadn't been able to protect her from her exhusband's infidelities.

All those old feelings came crashing back as he listened to seven-year-old Teddy, his surrogate nephew, declare that there was trouble at home. He didn't wait to hear what kind of trouble. He didn't stop to wonder why Cassie hadn't called herself. He only reacted, knowing in his gut that he'd walk through a blazing inferno for that woman if she needed him to.

"Ken, I'm out of here," he declared, already running. "I'll be back as soon as I can."

"You're going?" the manager sputtered incredulously as he tried to catch up, his arms pumping furiously. "What the hell are you talking about, Starr? We're in the middle of practice, not some Sunday-school picnic. You don't just walk out in the middle of practice. I don't care if it is spring training. That's all the more reason to buckle down. We've got our first Grapefruit League game next week. We've got a whole season ahead of us. These guys are playing like they ain't left the sandlot. You're supposed to be a leader, an MVP, for crying out loud. What the hell kind of example are you setting?''

''A bad one,'' he admitted dutifully, not slowing down. He'd grovel later. ''Fine me.''

Leaving Ken still lecturing and waving his arms, J.K accelerated across the practice field and went directly to the parking lot. He didn't even waste time getting out of his cleated shoes, despite the damage they were likely to do to his precious sports car.

Panicked thoughts sped through his brain as he made the familiar forty-minute drive in under twenty minutes. He wasn't sure what he expected to find, but it wasn't the serene picture that greeted him when he screeched to a halt in front of Cassie's house in the quiet Lake Worth neighborhood where Ryan had settled them before taking off. Teddy and a friend were sitting side by side on the front steps, elbows on filthy knees, chins in grubby hands. At the sight of the car, Teddy's face split with a crooked grin and they barreled across the yard, the friend lagging only a few paces behind an instantly animated Teddy.

''Uncle Jake! You came!''

He threw himself into J.K.'s waiting embrace. J.K. gathered the boy close, reveling in the sudden happiness that washed through him. He held Teddy in the crook of his arm as he anxiously scanned the porch and yard for some sign of Cassie. ''Of course I came,'' he said. ''I couldn't let down my favorite pal, could I? What's up?''

Instead of answering, Teddy turned to his friend. ''See, Billy, I told you. I told you he'd come.'' His arm circled J.K.'s neck possessively. ''He didn't believe me,

Uncle Jake. He said I didn't know anybody as important as you."

The full import of Teddy's words took a minute to sink in. In the meantime, like a man coming home after a long absence, J.K. examined the tiny stucco house with its flamingo-pink trim, neat yard and splash of bright red geraniums beneath each window. A purple bougainvillea struggled to climb a lopsided trellis. Only when he'd reassured himself that nothing seemed to be dreadfully amiss did his pulse begin to slow. Hunkered down, he turned Teddy to face him. "Okay, pal, where's you mother?"

Teddy took a step back and shrugged, blue eyes downcast, his expression decidedly guilty. "Inside, I guess," he mumbled.

"You guess?" J.K. said, beginning to accept the fact that Cassie hadn't needed him after all. Just to be sure, he persisted. "What's the emergency, Teddy?"

The boy's freckled cheeks flamed red. He stared at the ground, scuffing his sneaker in the dirt. "Umm . . ."

"Teddy?"

"I told you," he said with a defiant lift of his chin that was all too reminiscent of his stubborn, bullheaded father. "Billy didn't believe you were really my uncle. I had to show him, Uncle Jake. I had to."

Under J.K.'s stern look, Teddy's defiant mask began to slip. It was impossible, though, to miss the desperate yearning on his face. J.K. knew he should be furious. He knew Teddy needed a lecture, maybe even punishment, but first and most of all he obviously needed reassurance that somebody cared.

"Okay, sport," he said gently. "Here I am. If you guys have any baseball cards around, I'll sign 'em for you before I go back to practice, okay?"

Skinny arms circled his middle and he could feel Teddy's small, dirt-streaked body heave a sigh of relief. It brought a lump to his throat when Teddy whispered, "Thanks, Uncle Jake. I really, really missed you."

"And I really missed you, but don't thank me yet, slugger. We still have to talk about what's an emergency and what's not, okay?"

Teddy grimaced. "Yeah, I guess."

"There's no guessing about it. I'm going in to talk to your mom, while you say goodbye to your friend. Be inside in five minutes."

The walk to the front door was one of the longest J.K. had ever taken. It had been nearly a year since he'd seen Cassie. For a good bit of that time he'd been on the road, but he'd gotten back to Florida in the fall, right after the World Series and only weeks after her divorce from Ryan had been finalized. He'd wanted desperately to stop to see for himself that she was okay, but Cassie had made it plain that Ryan's friends were no longer welcome. Because J.K recognized the hurt that ran deep inside her, he'd given her space and time to heal. He'd called once, just to let her know that he was around if she needed him, but Cassie would never admit to needing anyone, least of all her ex-husband's best friend. She'd thanked him politely and hung up before he'd had a chance to say anything more. There were no shared jokes, no friendly teasing about his overly active love life, no hint of the old closeness at all.

The front door was standing open now and he could hear Cassie's cheerful, off-key singing coming from the kitchen. He listened and smiled. She never had been able to carry a tune worth a damn, but oh, how she loved to sing. He and Ryan used to kid her unmercifully, begging her to quit, threatening to drown her out with something more pleasant, like the sound of a lawn mower. She'd always told them to go right ahead. The grass needed cutting, anyway. Listening to her now filled J.K. with nostalgia and an odd stirring of tenderness toward sweet-natured Cassie Miles.

She looked anything but sweet, however, when she walked out of the kitchen just then and saw him framed in the doorway. The song died on her lips. She stopped where she was, her expression frozen. Her hands balled into angry fists at her sides. He ignored that and drank in the sight of her. She'd lost weight. In shorts that bagged and a shirt that hung loose, she looked to be maybe a hundred and five pounds of pure resentment. Her blond hair was caught up high on her head and shaggy bangs framed a face that seemed to be all gumdrop-blue eyes.

"Hi, Cassie," he said quietly, wishing it didn't hurt quite so much to see her look at him as if he were ten times more disgusting than pond scum.

"What are you doing here, J.K.?" The question was edged in ice and twice as hard. The Cassie he remembered had been all warmth and sunshine.

"It's nice to see you again, too, Cassie."

Only a man totally attuned to the quicksilver shifts in her moods would have noticed the subtle stiffening, the fleeting guilt that darkened her eyes at his barb. Cassie had been reared by kind, salt-of-the-earth parents who didn't insult guests in their home, not even a man she equated with everything that had gone wrong in her marriage. Still, guilt-ridden or not, her unwelcoming expression didn't soften the tiniest bit.

"How've you been, Cassie?" he asked more gently, worried by the weight loss, the dark smudges under her eyes, her pale complexion.

As if the question were a challenge, she drew in a deep breath. Her spine straightened perceptibly. "Fine, J.K. Teddy and I are just fine, if that's what you came to find out." Her words were emphatic and clearly meant as a dismissal. When he didn't budge, she continued to regard him warily.

Like a hunter stalking an uneasy prey, he took a cautious step closer. She didn't withdraw, but cast a disapproving glance at his feet. Suddenly conscious of the damage his baseball shoes could do the the carpet, he grinned apologetically and took them off. Standing before her in his stocking feet made him feel oddly vulnerable. "I think we need to talk," he said, awkwardly clutching the filthy shoes.

A dozen different emotions seemed to war on her face. Denial. Anger. Confusion. Fear. And more he didn't even recognize. She visibly fought for control, then finally asked, "Has something happened to Ryan?"

He supposed it was the obvious conclusion for her to reach, but the question and the raw emotions behind it were like blows to his midsection. He hadn't prepared himself to deal with so many still-unresolved feelings. Steering clear of the mine field, he said, "No, babe. It's your son."

Momentary panic turned her deathly white. She swiveled instinctively toward the porch and J.K. cursed himself for his insensitivity.

"Teddy's right outside," she said as if reassuring herself. Her tough guard dropped away. "I mean he was just a minute ago. J.K...?"

He touched her arm, then drew back at once when she flinched. "It's okay, Cass. He's there. I'm sorry. I didn't think. He'll be in in a minute."

She walked to the front door and looked out, her shoulders finally relaxing once she caught sight of Teddy. "What about Teddy?" she inquired, cool and barely polite again. "If you're here for Ryan, tell him to fight his own battles, J.K."

"This has nothing to do with Ryan. Or maybe it does. I don't know. Teddy called me, Cass. Out of the blue."

She looked stunned. "He called you? When? Why?"

"A little while ago, at the ballpark. Who knows how he came up with the dugout number."

She closed her eyes and apparent embarrassment flooded her cheeks with color. "It's still on the wall by the phone in the kitchen. I guess I never did take it down. I'm sorry, J.K. Ken probably pitched a fit."

He shrugged, downplaying the manager's reaction. "Ken enjoys snarling. You know that. It's no big deal."

"I don't understand, though. Why would Teddy call you?"

"Nothing catastrophic, though he claimed it was an emergency," he told her with the first hint of a smile. "As it turns out, he just wanted to prove a point to his friend. I gather Billy's new to the neighborhood."

She nodded, then shook her head in apparent bemusement. J.K. knew exactly how she felt. "What point?" she asked finally. "I still don't get it."

"That I was his uncle. I think maybe it was more than that, though. I think he must be missing Ryan."

Her expression, which had seemed almost friendly for just a heartbeat, instantly turned bitter. "Good guess, Dr. Freud. The last time his daddy called was when he passed through town three weeks ago on his way down to Miami. Judging from the length of the conversation, it amounted to hello and goodbye. Teddy went to his room right afterward and wouldn't come out. He still won't tell me what Ryan said to upset him so."

J.K had to swallow an oath. "Didn't Ryan stop by? When I saw him at the ballpark, I was sure..."

She cut him off with one succinct comment. "He had a date."

He did curse under the breath at that, then sighed. "I see."

"I'm sure you do," she said, building up a new head of steam. "Nobody knows Ryan better than you do, right, J.K.?"

"Cassie, rehashing Ryan's bad habits won't do anybody any good."

"Don't you try to placate me with that patronizing tone. You're every bit as bad as Ryan Miles." Once she'd started, she couldn't seem to stop. The anger boiled up and spewed over him in furious waves. "That's why you never told me he was fooling around on the road, isn't it? Do you all take a solemn oath of silence, is that it? Forget decency. Forget friendship. To hell with marriage vows. You all figure the women, those hot little bleacher bunnies, just go with the territory, right?" She ran out of steam finally and threw up her hands in a gesture of disgust. "You all make me sick. You're nothing but a bunch of overgrown adolescents."

For someone who hadn't wanted to talk, she'd managed to say a mouthful and every word of it filled with condemnation. J.K. accepted the hurled insults, but not the blame. "That's not the way it was, Cassie," he said with careful patience. "It killed me, what Ryan was doing to you and Teddy, but it was between the two of you. It wasn't up to me to tell you anything."

"Then maybe you should have reminded him once in a while that he had a family at home waiting for him. Would it have killed you to do that much, J.K.? Or isn't it macho to talk about wives and kids?"

J.K. winced. Locker-room talk all too often had more to do with the scoring off the field than on. He wouldn't admit that to her, though. Some truths were better left unspoken. There was one hard truth, though, that it was about time she faced up to. "Cassie, if you couldn't make him stay, then all the words in the world from me weren't going to make any difference," he said.

The blunt, untempered statement brought quick tears to her eyes. Her shoulders drooped in resignation and all the anger seemed to drain straight out of her. "You could have tried, J.K." she said miserably "Damn you, you could have made the effort."

Regret pierced through him. She would never know how hard he had tried, how Ryan had laughed at him for his feeble attempts to get him to ignore the feminine bounty that was available and go home to his wife and son. He wasn't about to tell her that now. She'd already been hurt enough and from what he could see the healing process was a long way from over. If heaping some of the blame on his shoulders helped her to cope, then he'd deal with it. What the hell, maybe there was something more he could have done. Maybe he wasn't blameless, after all.

"Cassie, isn't there something I can do to make things easier for you? You and I always could talk. Maybe we could go out to dinner sometime, like old times. I'm a good listener."

"I don't want your pity, J.K., and I don't need anybody to listen to me. I want to forget the past, not relive it. I thought I was doing real well until you walked in here and reminded me of everything. I guess I was overdue for an outburst. I'm sorry, though, for taking my problems out on you. Thanks for coming by to check on Teddy."

"Sounds to me as if you have a lot of anger left inside. If yelling at me helps, feel free. I've withstood far worse."

"No. I've said my piece now," she said, squaring her shoulders. "I'll speak to Teddy, too. He won't be bothering you again."

J.K. only barely resisted the urge to grab those pride-stiffened shoulders and shake her until she grasped how important she and Teddy were to him. They were like family, to all intents and purposes the only family he had. Instead of telling her that, though, he kept a tight rein on his patience and said, "I don't mind him bothering me, Cassie. I've missed you both. In fact, why don't you let him come back to the ball-park with me? He can watch practice, then I'll pick us all up a couple of hamburgers and bring them back for dinner. Hanging out with the guys might be good for him."

Cassie looked as if he'd suggested a rendezvous with the devil himself. Furious eyes blazed at him. "No! Absolutely not! I won't have him around that place. Not ever!"

The irrational outburst stunned him. "Cassie, be reasonable. The ballpark's not the problem. I'm not the problem. Don't you think it would be good for Teddy to have a father figure in his life? That's really what this call of his was all about. If Ryan can't be around, let me fill in. You know I love him."

He could tell he'd struck a nerve. She twisted the dish towel she still held in her hands, wrestled with a whole ton of maternal guilt, then finally shook her head. "Not you," she told him, evading his gaze. "Teddy needs someone, J.K., but not you. You'll just up and leave him, too. He doesn't need to be abandoned twice."

Even though he understood that her attitude toward him was all mixed up with her feelings for Ryan, the outright rejection hurt. He wasn't about to accept her decision as final, though. Not this time. Not now that he'd seen how badly she and Teddy needed someone in their lives, how lost and alone they both seemed. Not with all this guilt she'd heaped on him. And not since he'd realized in that split second when she'd walked out of the kitchen that he was still more attracted to her than he'd ever been to another woman.

That reaction probably should have been a warning, but to J.K. it was more like a call to arms. He'd never walked away from an attractive woman in his life. Flirting came as naturally to him as breathing. Cassie always had been a great target for practicing his technique. As long as she'd been married to Ryan, she'd been safe and she'd kept him honest, taking him to task for his flaws in a way most women never dared.

The decision to stay in touch firm in his mind, he could afford to back away for the time being, let her settle down a bit and get used to the idea of his coming around more often. "Okay, Cass. I won't press this time, but I will be back."

She shook her head, that haphazard blond ponytail bouncing violently. "Nothing personal, J.K., but don't come." She faced him down. "Teddy and I don't need you."

"A less confident man would take that as an insult, babe."

"I meant it to be one," she admitted, meeting his gaze with an unflinching stare.

He took one step closer, admiring the fact that she didn't retreat, even though he could tell she wanted to. He reached out a finger and touched her cheek. It felt like silk and it was still damp with the tears she hadn't bothered to wipe away. The pad of his thumb swept across her lower lip and he wished desperately that he had the power to still the trembling. Wished even more that he had the right to kiss her the way he'd longed to for one jealous instant the very first time he'd ever seen her. He'd felt like a heel then and he felt like even more of one now. Lusting after his best friend's wife, for God's sake. Maybe Cassie was right about him. Maybe he was every bit as bad as Ryan. Maybe he ought to walk out the door and let her be.

Still, he owed her.

"I think you do need me, sweetheart," he said quietly. "And until you prove me wrong, I think I'll just stick around awhile."

Without waiting for a reaction he turned and walked outside, pausing on the front steps to tug his shoes back on. He spotted Teddy hiding out around the corner of the house.

"Okay, sport," he called, beckoning him over. "It's time to face the music."

Teddy approached cautiously, his blue eyes every bit as huge and round as Cassie's. "I didn't mean to do anything wrong, Uncle Jake. Really."

"I know you didn't, but an emergency is something that's really, really serious. Something like maybe you're sick or your mom's hurt herself..."

"Or the house is on fire. I know to call nine-one-one for that."

"Exactly like that. Those are real emergencies. Anytime you need to see me, though, you can just call. It doesn't need to be an emergency. If you want to talk or maybe have a hamburger or toss a few balls around, you let me know."

He glanced up and saw Cassie in the doorway watching them, a frown on her face. "Your mom and I will work out the details, okay?"

Teddy flung his arms around his neck again. "Thanks, Uncle Jake."

"No problem, slugger," he said, raising his eyes to meet Cassie's disapproving gaze. "No problem at all. You might want to call me at home, though, instead of the ballpark. I have a machine that takes messages and I promise I'll get back to you right away. Your mom will put that number by the phone in the kitchen, where the ballpark number was." He strongly emphasized the past tense, while staring pointedly at Cassie.

The beginning of a smile teased at her stubbornly set lips when he said that. They both knew that Ken Hodges would develop an ulcer—and J.K. would wind up paying half his much-publicized, exorbitant salary in fines—if Teddy repeated today's interruption of the team's practice session. Heaven forbid he should ever get it into his head to call during a game.

"Will you take me to a game one day, Uncle Jake? Dad used to let me sit with him in the dugout sometimes."

"I remember," he said as the last trace of Cassie's smile vanished. J.K. took the hint and kept his response cautious. "We'll have to see about that one, though. Maybe one of these days, if you're real good and ask her nicely, your mom will bring you by."

She glared at him. He smiled back innocently. "See you two later," he promised, getting to his feet. "Take care of yourself, Cassie."

She nodded curtly and turned away. "Teddy, I want to see you inside right now," she called over her shoulder.

"I guess I'm gonna get it now," Teddy said with a resigned sigh.

J.K grinned at his attempted bravado. "I guess you are."

"I'm still glad I called you, Uncle Jake."

"Me, too. Let me give you a tip, sport. There's no point in trying to wriggle out of this one, but maybe if you just tell her the truth about why you called, she'll go easy on you."

"I guess," Teddy said doubtfully.

"Try it. Your mother's a reasonable woman."

He said the last loudly enough to stop Cassie in her tracks. When she whirled around to glower at him fiercely, he waved jauntily and climbed into his car. As he drove back to practice, he caught himself whistling. It was the same song Cassie had been murdering so cheerfully right up until that moment when she'd found him in her living room.

Two

There were millions of men in the United States, Cassie observed as she attacked the huge stack of dishes in the sink. There were thousands right here in Lake Worth. Why, of all of them, had Teddy called her ex-husband's best friend? The more telling question, the one she didn't care to examine too closely, was why it bothered her so much. It had been a week since J.K.'s unexpected arrival on her doorstep and she was still as jumpy as a June bug. She was also no closer now to understanding her violent reaction than she had been at the time.

Okay, so J.K. was a link to the past, a past she very much needed to forget. So what? They'd been good friends once. It was nice of him to worry about her, wasn't it? What was so terrible about the fact that he'd hotfooted it over in response to a little boy's call? Nothing, she admitted. It was a generous gesture.

Probably.

She couldn't forget, though, that J.K. was cut from essentially the same opportunistic cloth as Ryan. If she lived to be a hundred and ten, she would never permit another selfish, skirt-chasing, macho jerk near her and Teddy, especially not one as drop-dead attractive as J.K. Starr. Women would be swooning over the man when he was eighty. She'd even felt a guilty pang or two of fascination herself, especially when her marriage was falling apart and J.K. was rock steady beside her. But she was no fool. Any man could muster up compassion and sensitivity when he wanted to, for the short term. She had learned from her mistake. Now all she wanted out of life was to settle down to a nice, peaceful, ordinary existence with her son. Maybe, someday, that life would even include a man again... preferably one who hated baseball as passionately as she did.

"You scrub that plate any harder, you're going to wash off those little bitty flowers."

Cassie jumped at the sound of J.K.'s lazy, amused, Kentucky-bred drawl. His arrival wasn't totally unexpected, but it was every bit as devastating as she'd anticipated. The plate crashed to the floor and shattered. She shot a furious look at the man who was standing just outside the screen door. She opened her mouth, but before she could say an accusing word, he held up his hands in a placating gesture.

"Don't blame me," he said. "I'm just an innocent bystander."

"You weren't innocent the day you were born," she muttered, picking up the pieces and tossing them into the trash. Now that J.K. was actually here, filling the doorway with his broad shoulders and that sexy, end-of-the-day shadowed jaw, Cassie discovered that there was some perfectly ridiculous part of her that was glad to see him, relieved just to have an adult for company no matter his motives. She decided she'd better stomp on that part until it was well and truly dead. That meant resisting J.K.'s beguiling grin and his effortless charm. He was directing one of those magazine-cover smiles at her now. She steeled herself against the powerfully sexy effect, ignored the gentle and surprisingly familiar tug on her senses.

"Now that's a fine thing to be saying about the man who's going to take you away from all this," he said as he came through the door and settled himself on one of her kitchen chairs, his faded jeans molded tight, his baseball cap like worry beads in his strong, restless hands.

How many times had he done just that, she thought, regarding him warily. He'd always lingered in the kitchen while she cooked, chatting about inconsequential things, expressing interest in her observations, always making her laugh while they waited for Ryan to turn up. Now J.K.'s blue-green eyes were filled with that familiar humor and something more. A dare? Surprised, she realized the man was actually daring her to fight him. Welcoming the prospect on some instinctively feminine level, Cassie braced herself for the heady thrill of battle. J.K. knew exactly how to get her goat, knew her better, she'd thought sometimes, than her husband had.

"I don't want to be taken away," she said firmly, ignoring the contradictory fluttering of her pulse. Her chin tilted up a defiant notch, for her benefit as much as his. "And even if I did, you'd be the last man on earth I'd want taking me."

"Oh?"

There was an indulgent, arrogant tone to that single word that made her want to throw another plate straight at his cheating heart. "Go away, J.K." To her everlasting regret, the words came out more plea than demand. She was going to have to use more starch in her voice if she was going to win out against J.K.'s determined persuasiveness. "Go give one of those bleacher bunnies a break or have they all gone home to their mothers for the night?"

"I never did date jailbait, Cassie. I prefer my women with a little maturity and a lot of sass." His impudent gaze traveled over her insinuatingly. "Just like you."

"Your nerve never ceases to amaze me. Why'd you come back, J.K., when I told you not to?"

"Call me a masochist."

"More like a martyr. You've done your duty. You can leave now."

"And disappoint Teddy?" he said, pulling out the big guns, the ones guaranteed to shoot down every argument. With a skill most likely born of too much practice, J.K had zeroed in on her vulnerability more effectively than one of those heat-seeking missiles honing in on a moving target.

Her gaze narrowed. She busied herself by slamming a pot into the drainer, then picking up another one and scrubbing like crazy. J.K. waited her out.

"What does Teddy have to do with this?" she asked finally.

"I promised him ice cream."

She whirled around and planted sudsy hands on hips. This time there was nothing feigned about her anger. His arrogant disregard of her wishes was just one more indication that for all his good intentions, J.K. would always do exactly as he wanted. It was good that he'd done that. She might have softened toward him otherwise.

"You had no right, J.K.," she said evenly, proud of the fact that she wasn't screaming like a banshee.

"Cassie, what's the big deal?" he asked in a voice that seemed laced with genuine bewilderment. She didn't trust that innocent pretense for one millisecond.

"The big deal is that you didn't ask my permission. I won't have you making plans with Teddy without checking with me first. I told you that the other day."

He nodded slowly, his expression serious. "Okay, you're right. I should have checked with you first, but I got his message this afternoon and when I called him back over at Billy's, he sounded lonely. The invitation for ice cream just happened. I apologize."

The apology was meek enough, but the look in his eyes was anything but. It was the look of a man who knew exactly how to charm a woman into submission. He'd probably started practicing while he was still in the cradle. Still, she forced herself to murmur a polite, grateful response.

"I will remember next time," he vowed, reaching for her hand. The touch of callused flesh against her soapy hand was distractingly erotic. She began to forget all about the importance of keeping her defenses in place.

"As long as I'm here now, though, what do you say?" he prodded. "You always did like ice cream. Couldn't you go for a hot fudge sundae?" His voice dropped seductively. "Or maybe a banana split?"

Cassie's insides melted. She assured herself it was purely a reaction to the prospect of all that gooey hot fudge sauce running over triple scoops of chocolate ice cream and sliced banana and topped with a mound of whipped cream. She hadn't indulged in anything that deliciously decadent in months.

J.K. chuckled at her silence and kept up that relentless stroking of rough thumb over slick knuckles. "Tempted, Cassie?"

"You're not playing fair," she grumbled, yanking her hand away. She was definitely weakening and she wasn't one bit happy about it. No wonder women fell all over themselves to meet J.K. His style was smooth as aged whiskey and twice as intoxicating.

"Shall I call in my backup? If I get Teddy to work on you, we'll be at the mall in ten minutes flat."

She knew she ought to be made of sterner stuff. She knew she ought to protest his using her son to manipulate her, but the prospect of a treat for Teddy was something she couldn't bring herself to pass up. The tight budget she adhered to didn't often allow for such splurges.

"Maybe the two of you..." she began in an attempt to salvage her pride.

J.K. was shaking his head before she could complete the thought. "It's a package deal. You, Teddy and me. Think of it this way—if you're not along, I'll probably cave right in and let him have a double order of whatever he wants and then he'll be keeping you awake all night with a stomachache. You need to come along to keep us from overindulging."

She laughed at the ridiculous ploy despite herself. The tension that had knotted her shoulders for the past few days abated. She felt herself relaxing, looking forward to a brief respite from the dreary routine she'd settled into. It was just this one night and it was ice cream, for goodness sake. What possible harm could come of that?

"Okay, okay." She relented. "You win."

"Yeah!" Teddy's gleeful shout could probably be heard down the block. He poked his head out from behind the bush beside the back steps. "I told you it would work, Uncle Jake."

She faced the two of them indignantly, trying not to respond to their matching grins of satisfaction. "So, you two were plotting this, huh? Just for that, I'm going to order the most expensive thing they have."

"Do your worst, woman," J.K. said expansively. "I can't think of a better way to squander my money. Now let's hustle. A man could starve to death waiting around for you, right, Teddy?"

"Right. Hurry up, Mom."

"Can I at least run a comb through my hair?"

"Mom!" Teddy wailed impatiently.

"Give her a minute, son. Women aren't happy unless they've kept a man waiting. They think it'll show us who's boss."

"Don't warp my son's mind with your opinions of women, J.K. Starr."

"Why not? You seem to think I'm some sort of expert."

"I also think it's not something to be especially proud of," she retorted, then made a hurried exit to the sound of his laughter.

J.K. loved it when Cassie went all prim and proper on him. He knew just exactly how long to tease her to put the sparks in those blue eyes of hers. He was glad to see them back again. Standing up to him might give her back some of the self-confidence that Ryan's lousy treatment had apparently sapped right out of her. This ice cream thing wasn't totally for Teddy's benefit, either. Cassie needed to put a few pounds back on. By the time he was through, she'd be bright eyed, healthy and sassy as the dickens again.

While he waited he opened the refrigerator to grab one of the beers she and Ryan had always stocked. There wasn't one in sight. He settled for a box of grape juice, grimacing at the first sip of the excessively sweet drink.

"I'm glad to see you've finally decided to drink something healthy," Cassie said as she came back wearing jeans every bit as faded as his own and a blouse that matched the bluebonnet color of her eyes. She hadn't bothered with makeup, but her hair had been swept up in that ponytail that made her look about fifteen years old. She looked innocent and vulnerable and that powerful need to protect her swept through him again.

"No beer," he explained in a voice that was suddenly husky.

"No need."

He acknowledged the curt admission with a nod, trying to ignore the quick flash of pain in her eyes. He couldn't. "Cassie..."

"Don't say anything, J.K. It's all right."

"It's not...."

"I'm ready for that ice cream now," she said firmly.

He swallowed hard, wanting to say the right thing but not knowing whether he'd make things better or worse. When she was in this porcupine-prickly mood, maybe there were things best left unsaid. He nodded again. "Let's go, then."

At the mall they found seats in front of the crowded ice cream booth. "You save the table, Cassie. Teddy and I will get the ice cream. What do you want?"

"A banana split," she said without hesitation as Teddy ran off to get in line.

"Chocolate ice cream, extra hot fudge, no pineapple, just strawberries," he said.

"You remembered," she said softly. There was a look of pleased surprise on her face that made his heart ache for her. How many times had Ryan forgotten the piddling little things that two people building a life together should have remembered? Black coffee, two sugars, for instance. Or the fact that she hated pink, loved stuffed animals and wished on stars. He wondered what she wished these days.

"It's not that easy to forget, sweetheart. You used to have the cast-iron stomach and appetite of a truck driver. I lived in constant awe of you."

"Right," she scoffed. "Who was the one who considered four servings of the hottest chili in town to be a snack, then wondered what we were having for a main course?"

"Hot? That chili of yours was made for wimps."

"You ate four bowls, J.K.," she reminded him. "And it may have been mild when I fixed it, but you dumped an entire bottle of hot sauce in it. Even the bowl was pleading for mercy. Ryan took one bite and spent the rest of the evening chasing it down with beer."

The laughter in her eyes faded before she finished the sentence. J.K. reached out impulsively and squeezed her hand. "No sad thoughts tonight, okay? It's just us guys out on the town."

She nodded, but couldn't hide the shimmer of tears.

"Cassie . . ."

"Uncle Jake!"

J.K. glanced over and saw that Teddy was next in line. "I'll be right there," he told him, almost grateful for the interruption. For all he thought he knew about women, he was definitely at a loss when it came to giving comfort. Tears just about undid him. Cassie's tears made him want to throttle Ryan Miles. He brushed one errant teardrop from her cheek and felt something give way in his chest. "I'll be back in a minute with that banana split."

By the time he and Teddy returned, she was composed again. He set the ice cream in front of her. She toyed with it for the first few bites. J.K enjoyed watching the slow transformation from disinterest to enthusiasm. Even Teddy stared in amazement as the last bit of hot fudge vanished, carefully scraped from the sides of the dish.

"Awesome, Mom! You ate the whole thing!"

"It was wonderful!" she admitted with a sigh of pure pleasure. "Thanks, J.K."

"Care to go for two?"

"And spend the rest of the evening listening to you torment me about my appetite? Not on your life. What's wrong with you, by the way? You've barely touched your sundae."

"I've been too busy watching you," he admitted.

"How's the caramel?"

"Want to try it?" He held out a spoonful. Cassie leaned forward without hesitation. Her lips parted. And a jolt of pure electricity shot through him, startling him so badly he almost dumped the ice cream on the table. He was familiar with the hot, aching sensation, but not in connection with Cassie. For one brief instant he felt as though he were cheating with his best friend's wife. Then he remembered the divorce. He looked again into Cassie's clear, guileless eyes. Not even he could be low enough to take advantage of that innocence. He swallowed hard and with fierce concentration managed to get the ice cream into her mouth.

"Umm," she murmured. "That's almost as good as the hot fudge."

He shoved the bowl toward her. "Here, it's yours."

"J.K., I do not need your sundae."

"There's only a little left. Go for it."

"Maybe just another bite," she said, looking at him expectantly. Her tongue slid tauntingly over her parted lips. And another odd tremor jolted through him. He handed her the spoon with a sense of desperation.

"Be my guest."

When Cassie had finished his ice cream, she smiled in contentment. "I won't eat another bite for a week."

Worry began to nag at J.K. He sensed that there was more truth than exaggeration in the claim. Impulsively he said, "Oh, I'd bet I could talk you into a pepperoni pizza with mushrooms and green peppers tomorrow."

"Wow!" Teddy said, his eyes lighting up. "That'd be great! We haven't had pizza in ages. Mom tried to make one, but the crust was all soggy."

Cassie was shaking her head. "No, really. That's very nice of you, but I'm sure you have better things to do, J.K. Don't put your social life on hold for us."

He brushed aside the protest without missing the barbed tag line. "I can't imagine anything I'd rather do than spend an evening with the two of you. It's settled. You rent a video and I'll bring the pizza. I'll be by as soon as practice lets out."

J.K. was on Cassie's doorstep fully an hour before dark, much too early to eat dinner. He hadn't planned it that way, but practice had let out a little earlier than usual. He'd rushed home for a quick shower and a change of clothes, rather than hanging out with the guys. The next thing he knew he was pulling up in her driveway, pizza in hand. He refused to analyze the motive behind his rush or the unexpected way his pulse hammered every time an image of Cassie flashed in his mind.

Teddy came running down the block, his friend Billy hard on his heels. "Uncle Jake, you're early. Mom's not even home from work yet."

"Work?"

"Yeah, didn't you know? She has a job in some office. I think maybe she types or something. She promised to take me one day, so I could see where she works."

A hard knot of anger formed in J.K.'s stomach. "What do you do after school?"

"Go to Billy's. His mom's home all the time. Sometimes she bakes chocolate chip cookies for us. They're not as good as Mom's, though."

Despite Teddy's staunch declaration of loyalty, J.K. was certain he detected a forlorn note in his voice. He vowed on the spot that before long Cassie would be back home baking cookies, too. The means for accomplishing that eluded him for the moment, but he had no doubt he'd manage it. He'd be damned if Teddy was going to grow up as one of those lonely, latchkey kids who came home to an empty house or to some neighbor's cookies.

"You wanna eat the pizza now?" Teddy asked, regarding the huge box hopefully.

"Nope. We'll wait for your mom. Why don't you get a baseball and we'll play catch until she gets here."

The two boys were off like a shot to get the ball. J.K. sat the pizza on the hood of his car and propped one sneaker-clad foot on the bumper. He studied Cassie's house more closely. Once again he was struck by still more evidence that all was not going nearly as well with her as she'd wanted him to believe. He'd been fooled the past two visits by the cheerful flowers and the neatly tended lawn. He hadn't noticed that the paint on the house was beginning to peel in spots or that some of the tiles on the roof had broken loose. Thank goodness the rainy season hadn't started yet. Once it did, she'd have a living room full of water if she didn't begin the tile replacement soon. He'd call a roofer in the morning and have him begin work at once.

Pleased to have found something constructive that he could do to help, he put the repairs out of his mind while he played ball with the boys. Teddy had his father's natural ability. Though Billy was older and strong, he was still clumsy and within a half hour his frustration was showing. J.K. empathized with him.

"I didn't want to play catch, anyway," Billy said, blinking back big, fat tears. "I gotta go eat."

J.K. draped a consoling arm around the boy's shoulders. "Next time I come back, we'll try it again. All it takes is a little practice."

Billy sniffed. "Teddy's good and he's littler than me."

"Hey, it's a fact of life that sports are easier for some people than they are for others. That's not your fault, but giving up without trying, that would be your fault. You see what I mean?"

"I guess."

"You keep practicing with Teddy and I'll bet before long you'll be good enough to make first string in Little League."

He shrugged indifferently. "It doesn't matter."

"Do you like playing ball?"

"I suppose."

"Then don't give up. I'll coach you guys until you're the best in the neighborhood."

"Come on, Billy," Teddy urged. "Uncle Jake's the greatest. We'll be awesome."

"Okay," Billy agreed finally. "I really do gotta go now, though."

"Okay. 'Bye, sport."

Teddy waved. "See you tomorrow, Billy. Will you play catch with me some more, Uncle Jake?"

"You bet."

"What do you think you're doing?" Cassie asked, appearing seemingly out of nowhere, her voice strained. Surprised by her quiet arrival, he turned and realized that her car wasn't in the driveway. Since he wasn't prepared to deal with her abrupt tone, he focused on the absence of the car.

"Hi, sweetheart," he said, planting a kiss on her cheek and admiring the way she looked in the neat skirt and short-sleeved blouse that were a far cry from the shorts and T-shirts he'd usually seen her wear. "I like the duds, but you look beat. How'd you get here? Did you just snap your fingers and materialize?"

"I'm afraid extraordinary powers are a little beyond me. I owe my arrival to the city transit system."

"A bus?" he said incredulously.

"Don't look so stunned. That's why they have them," she said, still scowling at him.

"But you have a car."

"It's in the shop."

"It's been there a really long time," Teddy chimed in.

"How long?" J.K. said, his jaw set angrily.

"A few days. It's no big deal."

"When will it be ready?"

"Soon, I guess."

"Mom," Teddy protested. "The guy called yesterday, remember?"

"Is that true?" J.K. asked.

Cassie shrugged. "It's true. So what?"

"So why didn't you go get the car?"

"The bill was a little higher than I expected, all right? I'll pick the car up when I get paid," she snapped and stomped off toward the house. J.K. grabbed the pizza and followed.

"How much is it?"

"Dammit, J.K., I told you it didn't matter."

"It matters to me," he said, dropping the pizza on the kitchen table and reaching for his wallet.

"Put your money away."

"How much?" he demanded, peeling bills off and throwing them on the table. "Is that enough?"

"I don't want your money."

"Well, that's too damned bad. You're wiped out. I don't want you riding the bus. If it takes a few bucks to get your car out of the shop, I can certainly cover it."

Cassie picked up the money and threw it back at him. "I do not want your money, J.K., and I don't want you over here encouraging Teddy to play ball. Am I making myself clear?"

"You and that stupid stiff-necked pride of yours," he said, swearing loudly.

"Teddy, leave the room," Cassie ordered the wide-eyed boy.

"But, Mom . . ."

"Leave."

He inched closer to J.K. and tucked his hand in J.K.'s bigger one. "I'm staying with Uncle Jake," he said stubbornly.

"Don't you defy me, young man, or you'll spend the rest of the evening in your room. Now, go."

Teddy's lower lip trembled, but his back was stiff as he faced her. "You're going to make him go away, just like you did Dad. I know you are. I hate you! I hate you!" He whirled and ran from the room, leaving Cassie obviously shaken. Judging from her strained expression, she was also near hysterics.

As soon as Teddy was out of sight, she lashed out at J.K. "Don't you ever try to humiliate me like that in front of Teddy again."

"Humiliate you?" he repeated in astonishment. "Is that what you think I was doing?"

"It may not have been your intention, but that was the effect, just the same. I don't want him thinking I can't take care of the two of us. He's insecure enough since Ryan walked out. I won't have him scared out of his wits we can't afford the simplest little things."

J.K. felt the scared, desperate words slamming into his gut. "God, Cassie, I wasn't even thinking about that." He pushed his hand through his hair, feeling more helpless and frustrated than he'd ever felt before in his life. "I feel so damned lousy about the way things have turned out for you. I just wanted to help."

"I know you did," she said, her tone relenting slightly. "But that's not the way, J.K. The money's not important. We're managing."

"Managing," he repeated, as if the word were alien. Just *managing* wasn't good enough, not for her, not for Teddy. It offended his sense of order, his sense of what was right.

But with his hands tied, exactly what the hell was he supposed to do to make things better for them?

"I meant what I said about baseball, too, J.K. Don't encourage it. I won't have Teddy turning out like his father."

"Ryan's behavior had less to do with baseball than it did with his values. You're here to see that Teddy stays on the right track. Participating in a healthy, all-American game is not going to hurt him."

"Stop it, J.K. Just stop it. Teddy is my son, not yours. I know what's best for him. If you can't accept that, then stay away." Her voice was climbing and her lower lip quivered.

"Simmer down, Cassie," J.K. said gently.

"I will not simmer down," she said stubbornly, tears streaming down her cheeks. She swiped at them furiously. "You have no right coming over here and taking over. No right. We were doing just fine until you showed up. Now everything's such a mess."

Her too-thin shoulders shook with sobs. It was as if a dam had burst and for an instant J.K. stood by helplessly. Then he gathered her in his arms. "Oh, babe, don't cry," he pleaded, his voice gruff. "There's nothing wrong that can't be fixed. I promise you."

"You're wrong," she said, trying to break free.

"Shh," he said, holding her right where she was. "Trust me."

Her response to that was muffled. J.K. had a feeling it was just as well. Cassie was in no mood to trust anyone these days, least of all him. That might have been the very worst thing that Ryan Miles had done to her. A year ago Cassie had been the most open, trusting person he'd ever met. Ryan's betrayal had robbed her of her innocence, along with everything else.

Three

She'd lost it! Cassie wasn't sure what had come over her, but she had definitely lost it. Carrying on as if J.K. and Teddy were committing a crime just because they were playing catch didn't make a bit of sense. To top it off by throwing J.K.'s money all over the place was crazy. She had her pride, but that didn't give her the right to be downright rude in the face of yet another generous gesture.

She must be more exhausted than she'd realized from coping with all the changes. The tension of the past year had finally gotten to her, spilling out in this totally out-of-character, irrational outburst. She'd kept herself under control all these months for Teddy's sake and suddenly tonight she'd felt it slipping away the minute she'd turned the corner and seen J.K.

with her son. She supposed that the argument that had followed had been inevitable.

Still, she kept hearing Teddy's angry cry: "I hate you! I hate you!" It echoed again and again, every bit as awful as the day Ryan had said he was leaving, that he didn't love her anymore. No, she corrected, it was worse than that. Deep down in an unacknowledged part of her heart, she had anticipated Ryan's going. Teddy's intentionally cruel words had blindsided her.

"What have I done?" she murmured, her heart aching. "What have I done to my baby?"

J.K.'s arms, solid, warm and comforting, tightened around her. "It's going to be okay," he soothed.

If he'd promised something easy, maybe the moon, she might have believed him. This mess would never be okay. It only seemed to get worse. Even so, she welcomed the embrace, the awkward attempt to console. God help her, for just this one moment she needed his strength and, like Teddy, she wanted his easy reassurance. She sniffed as he rubbed her back.

"J.K., I'm making such a mess of things. I'm trying so hard, but everything I do is turning out all wrong."

"Shh. No, it's not. You're doing just fine. Teddy's a great kid. Kids and parents fight all the time. He'll calm down and then you can make him understand."

She swiped at a tear and grinned at him ruefully. "How am I going to do that when I don't understand it myself? I sounded like a lunatic for a minute there, and look at your money. It's all over the place." She kicked at a balled-up twenty-dollar bill. Others were scattered from one end of the room to the other. There must have been two or three hundred dollars in all, almost as much as she brought home in a week after taxes. Unskilled receptionists, she'd discovered, were in short demand and far from the top of the pay scale.

"Stop being so hard on yourself. The money can be picked up. As for the rest, even I can figure out what's going on here and I'm no expert. Just about the only thing I know about psychology is that you pay shrinks a lot of money to tell you awful stuff about yourself that you wouldn't take from your best friend."

"Then explain it to me, please, because right now I feel as though I've made an absolute fool of myself. Even more unpardonable, I've upset my son. He's just a little boy, J.K. He shouldn't have to try to guess why his mommy's behaving like an idiotic shrew."

He brushed the trail of tears from her cheeks. "Enough of that. Sit down and rest for a few minutes. Then we'll talk about it."

She peered at him suspiciously from the comforting circle of his arms. "Is this your sneaky way of sticking around after I've repeatedly banned you from the house?"

"Did you ban me?" he inquired innocently, pointing her toward a chair and giving her a gentle shove. "I don't seem to recall that."

"Selective hearing," she muttered. "Ryan had it, too."

He frowned. "Cassie, I wish you'd stop comparing me to Ryan."

"If the shoe fits..." she said, but her animosity was beginning to falter. She was beginning to remember J.K.'s good traits.

"It doesn't," he said adamantly. "Besides, in the long run, it's only going to confuse Teddy. You saw how he reacted tonight. He doesn't understand why you keep slamming doors on people he cares about."

She sighed. "I suppose you're right. Why do I feel the compulsion to do it then?"

He tapped her on the nose. "To remind yourself what a rake I am, so you won't be tempted to fall madly in love with me."

"What conceit!" she declared, but she couldn't help a wobbly smile. She must be the only woman in the country who wasn't half in love with J.K. Starr. How many of them would kill for this chance to have him lounging comfortably around the kitchen? Were they crazy or was she the blind one? She gave him a quick, surreptitious once-over, from tousled dark blond hair to cleanly shaven cheeks and on to flat stomach and solid thighs. His butt wasn't bad either, she noticed as he turned toward the refrigerator. The man was definitely sexy, she decided objectively. Maybe it wasn't conceit, after all.

"I prefer to think of it as self-confidence," he said modestly enough. The devilish twinkle in his blue-green eyes gave him away. "Do you want a soda or milk?"

"I'd take a stiff shot of Scotch if I kept any in the house."

"Scotch makes you weepy," he reminded her. "It's the last thing you need. Milk or soda?"

"Diet soda, if there's one in there," she said, chagrined by his all-too-accurate memory. She might have a cast-iron stomach when it came to food, but she had

no head at all for alcohol. One night she had fool-
ishly tried to match him and Ryan beer for beer only
to wind up turning melancholy after the second one.

"Hmm, there's no diet soda in here. Not unless it's
disguised itself in one of these little cartons. How
about apple juice instead? You can feel healthy and I'll
feel virtuous. Remind me to bring you a six-pack of
something stronger the next time I come over."

Cassie wasn't sure she liked the sound of that. She
wasn't very proud of her tantrum earlier, but that
didn't mean she wanted J.K. getting the idea he could
pop in and out around here at will. Having a pal like
J.K. would be risky business for any woman, but for
her it would be flat-out dangerous. Even if she was
willing to risk it for herself, she wasn't for Teddy. He
was the one who'd be hurt again in the end. Once
spring training ended, J.K. would head north for the
long baseball season and Teddy would know the feeling of being left behind all over again.

J.K. popped straws into the juice, handed one to
her, then pulled out a chair for himself. He turned the
back toward her and straddled it, his muscular arms
resting on the back. "Feel better?" he asked, watching her intently as she took a sip of the juice. The
sympathetic tone made her want to start bawling all
over again. She nodded.

"Then let's talk about it," he said.

"It?" Suddenly she wasn't at all sure she wanted
J.K. playing shrink with her emotions. As well as he
knew her, she feared his analysis might cut a little too
close to the bone.

"Don't play dumb with me," he chastised gently. "We're going to discuss that snit you worked yourself into a few minutes ago."

"It was not a snit."

"What would you call it?"

"A justifiable release of pent-up tension," she suggested hopefully.

J.K. actually grinned. "Sounds about right to me. In the future, you might want to consider taking a long walk instead. I hear it does wonders for stress and it's not nearly as disturbing to the neighbors."

"Very funny. I don't get it, though. I had a perfectly decent day at work. There were no major crises. I've finally figured out all the phone lines. I got paid. The bus didn't get stuck in traffic. Why did the sight of you and Teddy playing a simple game of catch in the yard turn me into some out-of-control crazy lady?"

"I can answer that with one word—Ryan."

She waved dismissively, unwilling to admit that there might be even a shred of truth in that observation. "You're not Ryan."

"Thank you for finally noticing."

She stared glumly back at J.K. and ignored the gibe. "He's been gone nearly a year now. I'm over him. He's history. Kaput. Nothing." In her head it sounded like the truth. Her gut told her it was a lie. Ryan Miles had been her childhood sweetheart, her first and only lover. Some women never forgot their first love. She was determined to. She glanced at J.K. and realized with a start that he could probably make her forget. In his arms... Whoa! She could feel the color flooding her cheeks and was grateful that J.K. would probably attribute it to irritation.

"I suppose you don't want to hear the line about protesting too much?" J.K. said, emphasizing the fact that so far she hadn't succeeded in forgetting anything.

She glared at him. "When did you get to be so obnoxious?"

"According to you, I've always been that way. Don't try charming me by calling me names. Stick to the subject."

"It's true," she said huffily. "I've accepted what happened. I've picked up the pieces and moved on."

"But you're still angry. Face it, Cassie, until you let go of the anger, you'll never be truly free of Ryan. Do you want him to have that kind of hold over you?"

"Of course not, but how am I supposed to go about doing that? Every time I see Teddy staring at a picture of his father, it breaks my heart. As for me, I can't get out of the supermarket without seeing Ryan's face on the cover of some tabloid or some sports magazine. It would have been hard enough if he'd been a nobody. Instead, he's got to have his best season ever last year. Then he tops it off by getting involved with that game-show bimbo and he's reached superstar status. The magazines can't get enough of him. Do you know he was on fourteen covers last year? *Fourteen!* The president wasn't on that many."

"Use the pictures for darts."

"Interesting notion. Don't you think that might get me arrested if I try it in the check-out lane?"

"Maybe all it would take would be one giant outburst. A little ranting and raving and crying. Did you ever do that, Cassie? Did you ever allow yourself to get really mad at him?"

"You mean before the last couple of days?" she said meaningfully.

"That was nothing. I mean a real hell-raising, dish-breaking fury?"

She shook her head. She'd cried herself to sleep more nights than she could remember, but she'd never raised her voice, not even at Ryan. She'd kept silent to avoid upsetting Teddy. It hadn't worked. He was obviously more shaken even now than she'd realized. "I couldn't," she told J.K. "I'm lousy at confrontation."

J.K.'s eyes rose in obvious disbelief. "You couldn't prove that by me."

"Okay, so I'm finally getting the knack of it," she said dryly. "At the time it seemed like such a waste of energy. Ryan was determined to leave. It wasn't going to change anything."

"Except, maybe, the way you felt. When I play lousy, you know what I do? I go back to the ballpark and get into the batting cage and slam balls for an hour or two. It doesn't change the way I played that day, but I feel a helluva lot better."

"How do you think Ken would feel if he caught me in his batting cage?"

"Don't ask. I'll tell you what, though. We'll make a deal. One night soon we'll get a baby-sitter for Teddy and you and I will stock up on all those sleaze tabloids, get drunk and burn the bunch of them. We'll even dance around the bonfire. How about it? Could be fun."

Despite herself, she giggled at the prospect. "Sounds like a pretty kinky date to me."

"Hey, that's the kind of guy I am."

She saw straight through the teasing, lighthearted tone and caught the serious caring behind it. It gave her an insight into J.K. she'd never had before. She'd always lumped him into the same devil-may-care league as Ryan, but perhaps she'd been wrong. There was an underlying decency that she'd been fighting to ignore. "I don't think so," she told him softly. "I think maybe I've misjudged you."

Her statement seemed to make him uncomfortable. He shook his head. "Don't go that far, Cassie. It's dangerous. My halo slipped off years ago."

She nodded thoughtfully. "Thanks for the warning. It only proves I'm right."

He shoved back the chair and stood up. "What it proves is that this conversation is getting way too heavy. Why don't you go have a talk with Teddy while I pick up another pizza?"

"You brought a pizza."

"It'll taste like cardboard by now."

"That's okay. Don't waste your money. I'll throw it into the oven and it'll be fine."

"I have an ulterior motive," he admitted with a guilty grin. "I cannot possibly eat pizza with apple juice. I'm bringing back a six-pack of beer for me and some sodas for you."

Cassie laughed. "Go, then."

He hesitated at the door. "You won't lock this behind me, will you?"

She shook her head. "No. I promise."

After he'd gone, she said softly, "Not tonight, anyway. But if I have a grain of sense, I will tomorrow."

Upstairs she found Teddy huddled on his bed, his favorite bear clutched in his arms. Ryan had given him that bear for this third birthday. For years it had been ignored on a shelf until Ryan left. Now Teddy was seldom without it at night. She sat down beside him. She could tell from the rigid way he was holding himself that he wasn't asleep. When she put a hand on his back, a sigh shuddered through him.

"I'm sorry, baby."

He sniffed and clung more tightly than ever to his bear, but said nothing.

"I shouldn't have raised such a fuss," she told him. "But sometimes I get scared."

"Scared?" The possibility seemed to intrigue him. "How come?"

"Oh, because your daddy left me and I want so badly to be a good mommy and make up for his having gone. But you know what scares me most of all? The thought that I might hurt you. I don't ever want to do that, Teddy. You're the most important thing in my life and I want so very much for you to be happy. Forgive me? Please."

He sat up and flung himself against her, his arms wrapping tightly round her middle, the bear caught between them. "I was scared, too. I don't like it when you yell at me. I don't ever want to make you mad so you'll go away like Daddy did."

Cassie's heart constricted painfully at the depth of his fear. "Listen to me, kiddo. There is nothing in this whole world that you could ever do to make me leave you or stop loving you. Nothing. Do you understand that?"

His head bobbed against her. "Did you make Uncle Jake go away?" he asked. Even though his words were muffled, she could hear the sadness and wariness behind them.

"He went to get another pizza, but he'll be back."

"You're not mad at him anymore?"

"No," she said softly, realizing it was true. Something had shifted tonight in her relationship with J.K. The fight had opened old wounds and left them raw, but for the first time she thought they might be healing. Maybe she and J.K. could be friends, after all.

"I'm glad," Teddy said. "Uncle Jake's the greatest, isn't he?"

"The greatest," she echoed. With the memory of his gentleness still lingering, she realized she actually meant it. She also knew that probably ought to scare the daylights out of her.

The pizza shop smelled of garlic and oregano. For J.K. it was one of the headiest scents in the world. He'd spent most of his teenage years hanging out in a place just like this one, the booths crowded with couples, the jukebox filling the air with country-western songs. Back home in his part of Kentucky, there hadn't been any place much fancier to go without driving all the way into Lexington. Giuseppe's, owned by a man whose real name was Billy Joe Callahan, had been like a second home to a kid whose own house was less than inviting. Billy Joe had encouraged him, cheering his victories and sympathizing with the defeats. He'd kept the high school team's baseball trophies along the back counter, and clippings about their games were tacked on a giant bulletin board. Once J.K. had turned pro, those clippings had joined the ones about the local team and the TV behind the bar was always tuned to J.K.'s games.

As he sat on a stool in the small Lake Worth shop waiting for his replacement pizza and listening to his country-and-western favorites, J.K. found himself wondering what it would be like to take Cassie home to Kentucky. What would Billy Joe think of the pretty little blond with the big-as-saucers eyes? And what would Cassie think of his hometown, a place so small a man could practically spit from one end of Main Street to the other?

Now, why was he thinking a fool thing like that, J.K. wondered, taking another sip of the draft beer that was ice cold, just like the ones at Giuseppe's. What had made him so nostalgic all of a sudden? Except for Billy Joe, he rarely thought of home and he'd certainly never considered taking a woman back there with him. He was still pondering that unexpected train of thought when a woman wearing tight blue jeans, a red Western shirt and a heavy, provocative scent of a zillion flowers slid onto the stood beside him.

"Hey there, Midnight," she said in a lazy drawl that sounded like home and lured like late night seduction.

His gaze wandered over her appreciatively. Her black hair was long and shiny, her lips red and tempting, just like the shirt which was opened one button below daring.

"I was watching you at practice earlier," she said in that low, sultry tone. "You were hot."

He acknowledged the double-edged compliment with a modest nod. "I had a good day."

Her hand covered his, blood-red nails against tanned male skin, turning up the heat a notch. "Honey, if all your days are half that good, the team will be in first and running away with it by the All-Star break."

He grinned at the enthusiasm. "You're a real fan."

"I'm a baseball junkie. RBIs and ERAs turn me on," she said provocatively, her bold gaze traveling slowly down his body.

There had been a time—probably not much more than twenty-four hours earlier—when J.K. would have given her a second glance. She was gorgeous and sexy and willing. Tonight, though, she just reminded him of too many others who trailed the teams in the hopes of scoring—forever or even for a night—with a ballplayer. She seemed a little pathetic. And the image of an impish blond with the spirt of a hellion wouldn't go away.

"Sorry, sweetheart," he said just as his order arrived. "I have someone waiting at home."

"Sure you couldn't stick around for just one more beer?"

He grabbed the pizza and six-pack and put a twenty on the counter. "Take the lady's drink out of that, too," he told the cashier.

She gave him a smile filled with regret. "I sure hope she's worth it, lover."

He grinned, surprised by the direction of his thoughts. "You know something, babe, I think she is."

Back at the house, he found Cassie and Teddy in the yard. She'd changed into paint-streaked shorts and a T-shirt that was faded from too many washings. She was definitely not trying to impress him, though he found the unassuming outfit ten times more appealing than the tight jeans and red shirt he'd just left behind. He watched for a minute as she and Teddy played catch. She was obviously trying to make amends, but she was lousy at the game. He chuckled as she chased down another ball that had been right at her fingertips.

Teddy came running over to him. "Mom's pretty bad at this, huh?" he said in a conspiratorial whisper.

"Pretty bad," J.K. concurred. "Maybe we should give her a break and go inside for pizza."

"What are you two conspiring about now?" she asked, sneaking up behind them.

"Conspiring?" J.K. repeated, looking offended. "Us?"

"That innocent act doesn't fool me. You two are up to something."

"We were just deciding whether to risk my car windows by leaving it within your throwing range. What do you think, Teddy?"

"I think you'd better put it in the garage," he said seriously, then broke into giggles.

Cassie was all offended dignity. She glowered at the two of them. "With a little coaching, I'd be just fine. Maybe even great," she boasted.

J.K. and Teddy exchanged looks. "Is that a dare?" J.K. said, stepping closer. "You're willing to submit to a little coaching?"

She backed away from him and the deliberate taunt. "No. I just meant . . ."

"Come one, Cass, let me teach you a few things," he said, his gaze locked with hers. An embarrassed blush tinted her cheeks pinks. "We could have a training session every night. By the time I finished with you, you'd have great hands."

She regarded him warily. "What did you have to drink while you were waiting for that pizza?"

"One beer and I guarantee it didn't go to my head."

"Maybe not, but I think I know where it did go."

"Why, Cassie Miles, are you flirting with me?" he asked, laughing.

Thoroughly flustered now, she scowled. "No. I mean I don't think so. Oh, for heaven's sake, J.K., let's eat this pizza before it gets cold, too."

As they walked into the house, J.K. wondered for the second time that night what was coming over him. He'd always liked Cassie, but this sudden desire to tease her with sexual innuendo was something new. He considered flirting second only to baseball as his favorite sport, but he'd never engaged in the most casual sexual banter with her.

Sure, but she'd been Ryan's wife then. Now she was free and he couldn't seem to resist. He enjoyed those sweet blushes and that hint of breathlessness in her protests.

Careful, though, he warned himself. Cassie wasn't in the same ballpark as the women he was used to. With her he could very well by playing with fire. As innocent as she was, they could both get burned.

"How come you're not eating your pizza?" Cassie asked when they'd been sitting around the kitchen table for a while.

He glanced down and realized that his first slice was still untouched, while she and Teddy had eaten nearly half the rest. Teddy had already excused himself and gone to his room. "I guess my mind wandered."

"I don't suppose I have to ask what you were thinking about. Who is she, J.K.?"

He regarded her blankly. "Who's who?"

"The new woman in your life. I've seen that look on your face often enough. It always involves a woman."

"Is that so?" He leaned back and stretched out his legs. He looped his thumbs through the waistband of his jeans. "What if I told you I was thinking about you?"

"I'd say you were being either gallant or evasive."

"Can't take the truth, huh?"

She tilted her head thoughtfully, still not convinced but apparently willing to consider the possibility. "What about me?"

"I was just wondering why I'd never noticed before how sexy you are."

She immediately blushed a fiery red. "J.K.!"

"It's true. You're a real heartbreaker, Cassie Miles."

"And you've definitely had a few too many drafts."

He shook his head soberly. "That's not the beer talking. If anything, I'm more alert than I've ever been."

She was slowly shaking her head. "Don't, J.K. Don't try to change things between us."

He reached across and touched a finger to her chin, enjoying the way her eyes flared wide with that first spontaneous hint of arousal. "I may have to, Cassie. I just may have to."

Four

Hanging out with Cassie was turning out to be a lot more fun than J.K. had anticipated when he'd first decided to start looking out for her. It was also playing surprising havoc with his hormones, which he definitely hadn't counted on. Restraint wasn't something he was all that familiar with, but if he'd discovered one thing over the past few days, it was that Cassie couldn't be rushed about anything. If he honestly, flat out told her he was developing this insatiable need to get her into his bed, she'd slam the door in his face so hard he wouldn't be able to pry it open again with a crowbar.

Smart woman!

Still, when she stared up at him with those wide, innocent blue eyes, yearning shot through him with a force that almost toppled him right over. He came to think of it as The Look. Guileless or not, it made him wary. It was every bit as dangerous as dynamite and a lot sexier. He began to stare at her lips the way a dieter stares at forbidden chocolate. It was getting harder and harder to resist temptation.

"J.K.?" Cassie said now, giving him The Look as they sat in the kitchen snapping beans for dinner.

"Mmm?" he said, fascinated by her. Why had he never noticed the way her nose turned up or that it had the cutest little sprinkling of freckles across it?

"Why are you staring at me like that?" she demanded.

"Like what?" he said, struggling for his own innocent expression. Her blush began at her chin and disappeared beneath her bangs. He loved it.

"You know," she muttered.

"As if I wanted to kiss you?"

She nodded, looking up finally. Her gaze clung to his and left him weak.

"Because I think I'm going to have to."

Her mouth formed a startled "oh." A handful of beans spilled to the floor. When she'd gathered them up she took a deep breath, then stiffened her spine, squared her shoulders and faced him head-on. "No," she said simply.

Perfect, he thought. There was nothing he liked better than a chase. At least she couldn't say he hadn't warned her.

"Yes," he contradicted, inching his chair closer. "I definitely think a kiss is in order."

"J.K." Her protest was definitely getting weaker and this time she didn't look away. She didn't scoot her chair away, either. "We talked about this."

"No, we didn't."

"We most certainly did," she said, waving a handful of green beans at him. "There's a chance, just a chance, that you and I could be friends, but no more. I'm not looking for a man in my life. Any man," she added emphatically, apparently to make sure he got her point.

"You need one," he contradicted.

"Says who?"

"Says me. You can't afford to have your car fixed. The house is falling apart. Teddy needs a father figure. I'm telling you you need a man in your life."

"And that's about the most sexist thing I've ever heard you say. What I need is a better job, not a man. Being a receptionist is no challenge. The people are okay, but the pay stinks."

"You shouldn't be working at all," J.K. insisted. "Teddy needs you at home. The right man would get your life back on track."

"Are you volunteering?"

"Yes, as a matter of fact."

"For what? Marriage?"

The word registered in his brain and exploded. "No," he said, too quickly. He didn't miss her smirk. She'd deliberately set him up. He equivocated. "I mean, not exactly. Cassie, be reasonable."

"I am being reasonable and practical. I can survive quite nicely without you or any other man. The bus gets me to work. If the roof leaks, I'll crawl up there myself and fix it."

"Right," he said skeptically.

"I can do it, if I have to," she said, matching stubbornness with pit-bull defiance.

"But you don't have to," he said, his patience slipping. "I told you I'd hire someone to fix the blasted roof and what does that have to do with kissing, anyway?"

"You brought it up."

"I brought up kissing. You changed the subject."

"It needed to be changed."

He groaned. "Cassie, I'm a dying man. Take pity on me."

An unwilling smile flitted across those luscious, tempting lips. "Men die from starvation, J.K., and you haven't lacked for kisses since you were twelve."

"Ten," he corrected.

"Ten!"

"I was precocious."

"Then it's definitely time for you to start tapering off."

He tilted her chin up with the tip of one finger. He could practically feel the shiver that ran through her. "Not yet. Not without one kiss from you. You're a free woman now, Cassie. And you're sexy and desirable. I don't think I can wait another minute to taste you, to see if your lips are as soft as they look."

There was an unmistakable flare of passion in her eyes. "No, J.K." There was a breathless desperation in her voice that was unmatched by the longing in her eyes. He went with the longing.

His fingers swept over the curve of her cheek to tangle in her hair. She swallowed hard, but again she didn't retreat. He had to admire her pluck. He could tell she was scared to death . . . of him, of the kiss, and most definitely of the implications. God help him, he ought to give her time. He ought to leave her alone. But . . .

"Just one, Cassie," he murmured, leaning forward until his mouth hovered over hers, their breath mingling. Then finally, slowly, inevitably, he closed the gap, not sure whether he was going to be smacked for his audacity, but willing to risk it for just one taste of those lips.

The first touch was feather light, a mere brush against silk.

The second savored, a gentle persuasion.

It was the third that set off unexpected skyrockets. Hungry, bold, demanding, the third kiss was a passionate declaration that left him breathless and shaken by its intoxicating message. Judging from the bewildered expression in Cassie's eyes, she was every bit as undone by the unexpected thrill of it as he was. Her small, slender hands, with their neat, blunt-cut nails, rested on his tensed forearms, lingering indecisively, not quite sure yet whether to cling or push him away.

He saw the precise moment she made her decision. There was no missing the slow rise of anger, the renewed quickening of her breath, this time stirred by fury. All that misdirected passion, he thought briefly, almost wistfully, as he braced himself for the inevitable explosion.

"Damn you, J.K. Starr!" she said, slamming down the bowl of beans so hard that half of them flew out. "You're exactly like Ryan. I was starting to believe you. I wanted to believe we could be friends, but you couldn't let it go at that. You had to try out your famous seduction routine and ruin it all, didn't you? What's the matter, were you getting out of practice? Or did you just think any woman—especially a lonely divorcée—would be grateful to be seduced by the great superstar jock? Not me, J.K." She was near tears as she shouted, "Not me!"

He waited quietly for the tirade to end. It was all steam and very little substance. He knew—and so did she—that no kiss that powerful was just a game anymore. It was a victory, a triumph. It was something a man didn't walk away from, no matter how it terrified him. She wasn't ready to hear that, though, and with a struggle he intentionally made light of it.

"That was a simple kiss, Cassie, not a seduction," he said, hoping he sounded clinically instructive and endlessly patient. Then he went and ruined it all by winking. He couldn't resist as he concluded, "When the seduction happens, babe, you'll recognize it and you'll want it every bit as much as I do."

He decided that was the perfect exit line, one to give her something to think about. Besides, it was time to pick up Teddy. He walked out without waiting for her reaction. She made sure he knew just how she felt, anyway. Before he reached his car, he heard the sound of glass crashing against the door, followed by the thump of something heavier and less breakable. The emotional clatter tempered by quick practicality made him smile.

"You're getting to her, J.K. You're definitely getting to her." One tiny little twinge of conscience told him that should make him feel guilty as hell, but it didn't. It made him want to shout at the top of his lungs.

Cassie stared after J.K., her emotions in a terrible tangle. He was wrong. This wasn't what she wanted from him at all. She didn't want to be kissed, not like he'd just kissed her. It made her want too many other things, things she couldn't possibly have—maybe never and certainly not with a man like J.K.

Stability, security, fidelity. Those were the qualities she yearned for. It sounded like the name of an insurance company and with J.K. the one thing she knew for sure was that there were no guarantees, no insurance for happily ever after. He'd kiss her today, woo her just the way he had all the other women in his life and then he'd abandon her the minute spring training ended. He wouldn't mean to. It was just the natural evolution of things with a ball player. An automatic, no-excuses way out of a sticky situation. She, better than anyone, knew the routine.

Experience had toughened her up, made her wary. Hadn't she tried to keep him away in the first place? She'd known he was trouble. But he'd kept coming around anyway, giving Teddy the masculine companionship he craved, ignoring her temper, chipping away at her defenses until she'd almost believed that she was safe with him. That kiss had snapped her back to reality. No woman's heart would ever be safe from J.K. Starr.

So, why had she responded when she knew the logical outcome? Why had that one long and dreamy kiss left her weak-kneed and hungry for more? Loneliness. That's all. Any kiss would have had the same breathtaking impact, she reassured herself. It had nothing to do with J.K.

Maybe she ought to experiment, kiss a few frogs as the saying went, just to prove that J.K. was no prince.

Maybe she ought to have her head examined.

Well, it wasn't something she had to figure out tonight. She'd been granted a reprieve. J.K. obviously had his timing down pat. Kiss and run. Give 'em something to think about. Well, she wasn't going to think about it for one second more. She was sitting in her kitchen all alone, just the way she usually did. When it came right down to it, nothing cataclysmic had happened to change the ordinariness of her life. Teddy would be home for supper any minute. He'd take his bath. She'd take her shower. And they'd both be in bed by ten. She took comfort in the promise of a perfectly normal routine.

"So, did you think about me while I was gone?"

Startled, she stared into J.K.'s twinkling eyes and groaned. "What are you doing here? I thought you'd gone home."

"And miss dinner, after I snapped all those beans? Not a chance."

"Then where did you go? Was that just another of your strategic maneuvers to throw me off guard?"

"Maneuvers?" he repeated with indignation. "I'll have you know that I do not *maneuver*. I went to pick up Teddy at the park."

Cassie moaned. What was happening to her? "Good grief," she murmured. "I forgot all about getting him."

"Fortunately, some of us are not so easily distracted," he taunted deliberately.

"Go to hell, J.K."

"Can I wait until after dinner? I'm starved. What are we having besides the beans?"

"We?"

"You did invite me over, Cassie. Did you forget that, too?" He placed a hand on her forehead. "Are you sure you're feeling okay? You seem a little warm."

Warm? She was burning up. She felt her pulse quicken. Tell him to go, she ordered her brain. It responded by saying, "Go. Stay. It makes no difference to me."

Liar! her brain shouted.

"Liar," J.K. accused, smiling confidently. He dropped a kiss on the top of her head in passing. "Don't ever try it on the big stuff, Cass. You're lousy at it."

"Not enough practice. Give me time."

"Cassie, there are not enough years in a lifetime for you to master that. Do I have time for a shower?"

She gulped. The very idea of J.K. naked did fascinating things to her heartbeat. Why had this blasted attraction smacked her between the eyes just when she was getting comfortable with J.K. again. "A what?" she said in a choked voice.

"A shower? I'm filthy. I came here straight from practice, remember?"

Her gaze traveled over the dirt-streaked, formfitting uniform. He was already unbuttoning the shirt, displaying a broad expanse of tanned, muscular chest. She'd seen J.K. bare chested before. It hadn't affected her like this. She swallowed hard, then cleared her throat. If it hadn't been so obvious she would have gulped down a glass of ice water as well. Better yet, she would have dumped it over her head and cooled off her hot thoughts. She cleared her throat again.

"Where are you planning to take this shower?" she asked. Despite the preparation, her voice squeaked anyway.

"In the bathroom. Care to join me?"

Her heart thumped unsteadily. "I have no intention of joining you in my or any other shower. Couldn't you go home and take one?"

"And be late for dinner and have you fussing at me?"

"I wouldn't fuss," she vowed breathlessly.

"I don't want to chance it. I figured practice might run late tonight. I've got a change of clothes in the car. I'll be right back."

The minute he walked through the door she began fanning herself with the magazine he'd brought in with the mail. The kitchen had gotten downright steamy in the past few minutes and she had yet to turn on the stove. What was he trying to do to her?

Don't be naive, she told herself. He was trying to rattle her.

And succeeding admirably, she had to admit, dropping the magazine and fighting for composure the second she heard him approaching the back door. She was not about to let him see how well he was doing. J.K. could flirt and tease all he wanted, but she was every bit as tough-minded as he was. She could withstand his assault. Sooner or later he'd tire of it and move on to someone who was easier prey.

The prospect depressed her. After he'd gone to the bathroom to shower she tried singing to cheer herself up, but the only songs that came to mind were country ballads about star-crossed lovers. She gave up, only to hear J.K. in the shower belting out the lyrics of a Kenny Rogers tune that always reminded her of Ryan. Terrific! Now she was going to get really depressed.

But she didn't. After a few minutes of waiting for the nostalgia to settle in, she realized that she wasn't thinking about Ryan at all. She was thinking about J.K's kisses and how very much she'd like to experiment some more. She was envisioning his body, sudsy and slick and hard. Oh, my, she thought, fanning frantically and to no avail.

"Talk about jumping from the frying pan into the fire," she muttered under her breath.

"Hey, Mom, how come you're talking to yourself?" Teddy asked, standing in the doorway.

"Because I'm losing my mind," she retorted. "Come give me a hug and help me save my sanity."

Teddy reluctantly submitted to the hug, then squirmed free. "What's for dinner? I'm really, really hungry."

"You are always really, really hungry. We're having spaghetti and fresh green beans."

Teddy made a face. "We just had spaghetti last night."

"It was two nights ago," she said wearily. "I thought you loved it."

"I do, but not every night."

"What's this?" J.K. interrupted, still bare chested but dressed in clean running shorts and rubbing a towel over his still-damp chest. Cassie's gaze locked on the dark blond hair that arrowed down to the elastic waistband of his shorts. She had to force herself to listen to his conversation with Teddy.

"You're tired of spaghetti?" he said, his expression astonished. "How do you expect to grow up to be the best ballplayer ever to graduate from a Lake Worth high school if you don't eat all this healthy stuff?"

Teddy looked skeptical. "You like spaghetti?"

"I eat it every chance I get, especially if your mom makes the sauce."

"She doesn't make the sauce anymore. She says she doesn't have time and that the stuff that comes in the jar is just as good."

J.K. regarded Cassie intently, but he kept up the valiant pretense. "It is just as good. Go wash your hands."

Teddy retreated without a battle.

"Thanks, J.K."

"I gather he's getting a pretty steady diet of this."

"It's nutritious and easy and I don't want to discuss it."

He held up his hands in a placating gesture. "Fine. I won't bug you," he vowed, tugging an out-of-shape team T-shirt over his head. Cassie wasn't convinced by the promise. Sooner or later he was going to start pestering her about money again. She appreciated his concern, but it was none of his business and she was getting very tired of telling him so.

Teddy ate his dinner without complaint, mimicking everything J.K. did to doctor up the spaghetti that Cassie suddenly found tasteless. They sprinkled on a heavy coating of Parmesan, added some hot peppers and mixed in the green beans.

"Wow! This is radical," Teddy said when he took his first bite. His eyes were watering from the peppers.

Cassie caught J.K.'s eye and grinned. "Hot enough for you, too, J.K.?"

"Better," he said. "Next time I'll toss in a little more oregano and garlic while it's simmering."

"Maybe next time you should be the one making it from scratch," she said, unable to keep an edge from her voice.

J.K. didn't rise to the bait. "Why do that when all it takes is a little ingenuity to fix this right up? Now, why don't you go sit in the living room and put your feet up, while Teddy and I do dishes."

Cassie stared at him, startled by the thoughtful offer. When J.K. was like this, it was all too easy to forget the danger of letting him get too close to her or to Teddy. Just look what had happened earlier, when she'd let down her guard. The man had practically kissed her senseless. She was about to object when she glanced at Teddy. He was nodding enthusiastically. "I can dry real good, Uncle Jake."

"I'm sure you can," he said, getting up and gathering the dishes from the table. "Go on, Cass. Leave us men to our man talk."

"Just don't offer him a cigar," she warned.

"Got it," he said, chuckling. "Any other ground rules for this occasion?"

"None I can think of."

"Then go."

She appreciated the gesture. She really did. But the minute she was in the living room, all alone, she felt lonely. She could hear the happy sounds of J.K. and Teddy at work in the kitchen and she wanted to be a part of it. She convinced herself to stay where she was. It wouldn't do to get too used to having J.K. around the house, doing chores, teasing Teddy, helping her. It certainly wouldn't be wise to pretend they were a real family.

But, oh, how the idea was beginning to tempt! It was getting harder and harder to keep J.K. at arm's length, even though she knew that in the long run it was for the best.

J.K. sent Teddy to take his bath, then went into the living room. He found Cassie curled up in a corner of the sofa, her feet tucked under her, her head on the armrest. She was sound asleep, her cheeks flushed, her hair fanned out in tempting disarray.

Unable to help himself, he went to hunker down beside her. An increasingly familiar tug made him ache to hold her in his arms. She was worn out and, again,

he was struck by a helpless anger that she had to work
so hard and for so little. Teddy's unwitting revelation
about the spaghetti had infuriated him. Sure, they
weren't about to starve to death, but the constant cost-
cutting measures were demeaning and unnecessary.
He'd seen the published reports of the deal Ryan had
struck with the new team. It had been in the millions.
That was more than enough to support Cassie and
Teddy in this modest little house. Hell, he could have
moved them into a Palm Beach mansion, complete
with pool and housekeeper. There was no reason for
them to be struggling so just to make ends meet.

Unless Ryan wasn't getting the alimony and child
support payments to them on time. As soon as the
notion entered his mind, he knew that had to be it.
Ryan had always been a big spender. No matter how
much he had, he always spent more. His much-
publicized generosity with lavish gifts was one of the
reasons he'd had so many women chasing after him,
even when he'd been married. More than once, he'd
spent money on his friends while leaving Cassie to
cope with the household expenses on the bank ac-
count leftovers.

It took everything in J.K. to keep him from going to
the phone and placing a call to Miami to tell Ryan
what a no-good, lousy son of a . . . Forget it. Cassie
wouldn't thank him for the interference and her pride
would never allow her to admit—especially to him—
that Ryan was late with the payments. She'd been embarrassed enough when J.K. had overheard her argu-
ing with Ryan for enough to pay the utilities one
month. The night before that incident he'd seen Ryan

lose a thousand dollars in a poker game without blinking, money that obviously should have gone toward the overdue electricity and phone bills.

Since Cassie seemed determined to cover for Ryan's bad habits, he would just have to find his own subtle ways of helping out, nothing as overt as trying to hand her cash again. She'd made it plain how she felt about that. But surely he could think of something else.

In the meantime, though, he wanted to get her into bed. Alone, he thought with a sigh of regret. Much as he wanted her, it was still too soon and she was far too exhausted. He scooped her into his arms, his breath catching as she snuggled against him, innocently tempting him. As he carried her through the house to her room, she burrowed her head into the crook of his neck, her breath a hot whisper against his flesh. Desire arrowed through him with an intensity that almost rocked him off balance.

"Oh, Cassie," he muttered, his voice husky as he tugged down the comforter on her bed, spilling her crazy collection of stuffed toys onto the floor. He gently placed her on the fresh sheets, then picked up a ragged, long-eared bunny and tucked it in beside her. He wavered on the issue of undressing her, then wisely decided against it. He had only so much willpower and it was already being tested to the limits.

"What are we getting ourselves into here?" he said, staring at her with longing.

She stirred sleepily. "J.K.?"

"Shh, sweetheart. Go back to sleep." There was an urgency underlying the request. Asleep, Cassie was provocative enough. Awake, she'd be dangerously irresistible. And he needed to get out of here tonight before they made a mistake from which neither of them would ever recover.

Five

The spaghetti incident, on top of a few other alarming signs, put J.K. on the alert. His protective instincts rallied, fueled by his overwhelming desire to bolster Cassie's spirits, to see her smiling again instead of worn out and blue.

Not that he was being totally altruistic, to be perfectly honest. He just recognized the fact that not even he could seduce a woman who didn't have the energy to resist him. When they finally wound up in each other's arms, he wanted Cassie every bit as spirited and passionate as he knew she was capable of being. He decided to turn detective to see just how bad things really were.

The next few times he went to get something to drink from Cassie's refrigerator, he took stock of the scanty contents. What he discovered was pitiful. There were a couple of containers of leftovers, a package of dried-out cheese, sandwich meat for Teddy's lunches, a few eggs, a carton of milk, some juice, lettuce and the usual assortment of condiments. One cupboard held peanut butter, bread, a few canned goods, a box of spaghetti and a bag of cookies. On Thursday night, increasingly worried, he stole a glance into the freezer. It was discouragingly empty as well, except for a couple of trays of ice cubes, two frozen dinners that looked about as appetizing as dog chow and some frozen orange juice. He slammed the door, wishing he could slam his fist into Ryan's face instead.

The time had definitely come to take action. He spent the whole day Friday thinking about it. Unfortunately, his pitching went to hell as a result. He blew more three-two counts than he had in all of his previous seasons of play combined. He actually walked in a run in the first inning. After taking about as much as he could of J.K.'s disastrous inning and a third, Ken delivered an ear-blistering lecture at the mound and yanked him. To add insult to injury, he replaced him with a kid who'd just been called up from the minors the day before.

"I don't know what kind of burr you've got stuck in your behind, but see to it that it's gone by this time tomorrow," Ken growled, stalking him back to the dugout. "The way you're playing, you might as well be back on the farm team. What the hell kind of leadership is that? I've got green kids out here pitching better than you."

The charge hurt, mostly because it was valid. "I won't make excuses, Ken," he said. "It was my mistake. I've got a lot on my mind."

"Some woman, you mean. I've seen it time and again. Some guy makes MVP a couple of times, gets a little publicity and bingo, he can't concentrate because his mind ain't on the game. Believe me, Starr, there ain't a woman in the world worth blowing your career over."

"Maybe one," J.K. said to himself as Ken, satisfied with having made his point, stomped off to sit at the other end of the bench. Cassie was worth every ounce of energy he had to spend on her. Why the hell hadn't Ryan realized that before it was too late?

As he tried to figure out his friend's stupidity, recalling all the great times the three of them had had together, the solution to Cassie's food problem finally came to him. It was so simple he couldn't imagine why it hadn't occurred to him earlier. He'd casually way lay her in the store, add a few extras to what she picked up, then pay for it all, swearing they'd divvy up the bill later. It was perfect, absolutely foolproof.

After all, he theorized as he looked for flaws, it wouldn't be the first time they'd wound up grocery shopping together. He and Ryan used to go with her occasionally, dropping junk food into the cart while she overloaded it with fruit and vegetables. They always left with the cart piled high. If his suspicions about money being tight were valid, he'd be able to tell at once just by looking into her grocery cart.

Tonight was the perfect time to try out his plan, too. It was Friday and Cassie had always shopped on Fridays, stocking up for the barbecues and impromptu parties Ryan liked to throw on the weekends after the games.

As soon as he'd showered and dressed, J.K. headed for her neighborhood supermarket. It was five-twenty. Cassie ought to be on her way home from work just about now. He waited for her in the parking lot for a while, then went inside. He stationed himself in the produce section, lingering over the oranges and apples for so long he began to draw curious glances from the help.

With some sort of ESP that he seemed to be developing where Cassie was concerned, he knew the instant she walked into the store. By the time she turned down the produce aisle, sashaying along in a cute little dress that skimmed her knees and showed off her figure, he was fingering a head of lettuce as if it were a ball he was getting ready to pitch on a full count. He waited expectantly for her to discover him.

She stopped in front of the tomatoes, picked up and discarded several, glanced at the price posted on the counter, sighed and took two steps to her left and began examining the lettuce. When she reached for a head, J.K. reached for the same one. Their fingers collided. Cassie began a quick apology, then looked up. A spontaneous, heart-melting smile broke across her features.

"J.K., what are you doing here?"

He bounced the lettuce idly in the air. "I was in the mood for a salad. What about you?"

"I always pick up the groceries for the week on Friday."

"Of course," he said. "I should have remembered. Everything going okay? How was your day?"

"Fine."

"Teddy?"

She regarded him suspiciously. "He's great. You just saw him two nights ago."

Whoops! He'd been so busy being nonchalant, he'd forgotten to use his brain. He glanced toward her still-empty cart and shifted his plan into action. "You haven't gotten much yet."

"I just got here."

"Mind if I shop along with you? You can give me some advice."

One brow arched deliberately. "Advice?"

"You know, about brands and stuff."

"I don't think lettuce comes in brands."

"Sure it does," he improvised hurriedly. "What we have here is your basic iceberg lettuce." He bounced it gently, then put it back and reached for another package. "Now there's also your endive, a little bitter for my taste. Maybe some Boston bib lettuce. What do you think? Maybe I should just go for spinach, instead. Spinach makes a great salad, don't you think?"

She laughed. "I think you're crazy. Nice, but definitely wacko. Do you have a similar problem with the tomatoes?"

"Indeed. We have beefsteak. These aren't looking too hot after that freeze back in January. Notice how they've gassed them to make them ripe. Nothing but mush. The plum tomatoes. I'm not so sure about those. I've never much liked them. But these," he said, lowering his voice to a seductive purr. He met her gaze as he held out a container of perfect, ripe cherry tomatoes. "These look just right . . ."

He watched the pulse in her neck begin to beat more rapidly. "For a salad," he concluded.

This was turning out to be more fun than he'd anticipated. Cassie was clinging almost desperately to her cart. She blinked and took the cherry tomatoes and placed them into the cart. He doubted she was even aware of it. "I don't think you need me for this," she said, her voice oddly husky. "You're doing just fine."

"But we haven't gotten to the salad dressings."

"J.K., in all the time I've known you, I have never seen you use anything except Italian dressing."

"But even with Italian there are so many choices," he protested.

"I have great confidence that you'll be able to make a selection on your own. Read the labels. Check out the herbs in the bottom of the bottle. Shake it. You can do it," she said, giving him an encouraging pat.

"Are you so sure? Practically since the day we met, you've been accusing me of letting indecisiveness ruin my love life."

Her gaze turned skeptical again. "What does your love life have to with this?"

"Nothing, exactly," he admitted candidly. "It's just indicative of a definite character flaw, isn't that what you've said?"

She regarded him incredulously. "So, because I think you'll never settle down with one woman, I'm also supposed to believe you can't decide among the various brands of Italian salad dressing."

He smiled cheerfully. "That's logical, isn't it?"

"That's bull—" She caught herself and quickly amended, "That's baloney."

"So you won't help?"

"Oh, I'll help, all right. By the time I'm finished with this lesson, you'll know every ingredient in every salad dressing on the shelf. Never let it be said that I allowed you to flounder through life not knowing how to fix a proper salad. Let's go."

"Great," he said and quickly dropped a couple of heads of lettuce and two more little baskets of tomatoes into her cart.

"Where's your cart?" she asked.

"Oh, I'm not getting that much. I might as well share yours. Do you want some fruit before we move on?"

"Just a couple of bananas for Teddy's lunch box."

"No oranges? You always loved oranges."

"They're too expensive right now. The freeze hit the groves up in Orlando pretty hard."

"Just take a couple. See, these are from California. You need your vitamin C. How much can three oranges cost?"

"Ninety-nine cents."

"A bargain, really. Just think about it. These little suckers flew all the way across country for thirty-three cents apiece."

"J.K.," she protested, but he'd already turned the corner and planted himself in front of the meat counter.

"How about a couple of steaks? The sirloin looks good."

"It's not in my budget," she said, her amusement visibly beginning to fade.

J.K. wasn't daunted. "They're on sale."

"No steaks."

"Hamburger, then. You used to make the best hamburgers. Maybe we ought to organize a barbecue this weekend. You know, the way we used to. What do you think? I'll invite a few of the guys and their wives. It'll be fun. They ask about you all the time."

"The last thing I want to do is spend an evening with Ryan's old pals. Come on, J.K., what is this all about?"

"What?"

"You are no more in here to buy stuff for a salad than I am to buy prime rib. What's the story?"

He hadn't prepared himself for a direct confrontation. He knew darn good and well that Cassie's pride would be shattered if he said anything directly about her financial situation. She'd rub his nose in that package of hamburger, then stalk off and leave him to explain the mess to the manager. Maybe he could turn this around simply by inviting himself over for dinner again and offering to bring the food.

"Maybe I was just angling for another dinner invitation," he ventured.

"And maybe you wanted to fly to the moon. Get real. You've dropped in for dinner five times in the last two weeks. You didn't grovel for those meals in the middle of the supermarket."

"I forgot my manners. I figure it's payback time. Besides, I enjoy your company and you do make great hamburgers. I'll grab the fixings and you cook again tonight. Consider it repayment for the meals I've been bumming the last couple of weeks. How about it? Or I could cook, if you're too wiped out. I can manage hamburgers."

The last trace of amusement vanished. "You never give up, do you?" she said wearily.

"I don't know what you mean."

"In a pig's eye. Look, I appreciate what you're trying to do here, but you're wasting your energy. I won't take money from you."

"I'm not trying to give you money."

She waved the two-pound package of ground round at him. "Okay. I won't take meat from you." She glanced in the cart and realized just how busy he'd been. "Or lettuce. Or tomatoes. Or California oranges. Am I getting through that thick skull of yours yet? I'll see you around, J.K. Maybe you can stop by to see Teddy over the weekend. He says I throw like a sissy."

Head held high, she made a quick turn onto the cereal aisle. Something inside J.K. snapped at the sight of that proud, stubborn posture. He caught up with her in front of the corn flakes and dumped an armload of meat and chicken into her cart. She whirled on him with startled indignation. He didn't care. He was ready for the outburst she was bound to make, looking forward to it, in fact. She'd been suffering in silence long enough. It was about time she got mad. Blowing off steam at him was a start. They'd tackle Ryan together.

"What do you think you're doing?" she snapped.

"Seeing to it that you and Teddy get a proper meal for a change. You're through living on spaghetti."

"There's enough food there for half a dozen meals and I don't want any of it," she fumed.

He leaned across the cart and stared her down. "Think about Teddy, for once, instead of that damned obstinate pride of yours." He decided to go for broke and lay it all on the line. "When was the last time Ryan sent you child support money, Cassie? Have you talked to his lawyer about it? Or are you just struggling quietly along?"

"Dammit, I don't want to hear this," she said, stalking off empty-handed. "Drop it, J.K. You have no right."

He grabbed her cart and caught up with her, trapping her next to the peanut butter. He grabbed the biggest jar on the shelf and defiantly tossed it into the basket. "I care, Cassie, that gives me the right," he said, adding a jar of grape jelly. "I'll be damned if I'll sit by and watch you starve yourself to death and scrimp to put a meal on the table for Teddy, when Ryan could afford caviar on the Riviera for the two of you."

"You have nothing to say about it. This is my life, J.K. Starr," she shouted. "Stay the hell out of it!"

"I will not," he said, suddenly aware that shoppers had stopped dead in the aisles to stare at the scene. He abandoned the cart, grabbed Cassie by the arm and propelled her out of the store.

"What do you think you're doing now?" she said, resisting him.

"Taking you someplace where we can sit down and discuss this situation rationally. Don't fight me, Cassie, or I'll carry you."

Her eyes widened. "You wouldn't dare."

"Test me."

They matched stares for several tense seconds before she finally said, "J.K., please, there's nothing to discuss. I have a job. I can support Teddy and me just fine. I don't want your money, your meat or your meddling. I sure as hell don't want your pity."

"Sorry, babe. Pity has nothing to do with it. I've walked away from a lot of responsibilities in my lifetime, but not this one."

She glared at him, sparks in her eyes, but her voice stayed soft. "You are not responsible, J.K. This is not your fault."

"That's not what you were saying a couple of weeks ago. You couldn't wait to heap the blame on me then."

"I was wrong, okay? I should have kept my big mouth shut. If I'd known this was going to happen, I would have. I wanted to blame someone for what had happened and you were handy. You told me yourself, though, that it was up to me to keep Ryan from walking out and you were right. It is also up to me to get him to face up to his responsibilities. I seem to be failing at that, too. I don't know what I could do differently, but it's my problem, not yours."

J.K. shook his head. "No, honey, I was wrong about that, too. It's Ryan's problem. He's the only one who could make the decision to stay or go and not a thing you or I could have said could have influenced him. As for the money, he's a man who'll always do exactly what he wants to, regardless of the pain it causes. Maybe it's going to take hauling him into court to get him to wake up.''

She shuddered visibly. The color drained out of her cheeks. ''And have the story on the front page of every sleazy magazine on the rack? No, thank you.''

''Just the threat would probably do it. He doesn't want that kind of publicity any more than you do.''

''For Teddy's sake, I'm not willing to risk it. Now, if you don't mind, I do have groceries to buy and a dinner to fix.''

''Stop running away from this, Cassie. I'll take you out to dinner. We'll talk it out.''

''I do not want to go out to dinner and I don't want to spend another minute talking about this.''

''You're just being pigheaded.''

''Talk about the pot calling the kettle black. You're not exactly being a paragon of compromise.''

''You want compromise, we'll compromise. I'll buy your groceries this week and you can buy them next week. We'll take turns cooking. You'll be doing me a favor. I'm lousy in the kitchen.''

''It's probably the only room in the house where you are,'' she grumbled under her breath.

''Thanks for the compliment.''

''I meant it as an insult.''

''Whatever. So, Cass, what's it going to be? Do I buy the groceries or do I talk to Ryan?''

''That's blackmail.''

''Not a pretty word, but fairly accurate.''

She regarded him helplessly. ''J.K., what exactly will it take to get you to drop this savior role you've adopted? I will say this one last time. I do not want to be protected. I do not want to have my roof fixed. I do not need a father figure for my son. And I do not need to be fed like some sickly calf you're hoping to fatten up for market."

He flinched at her interpretation of what he was trying to do. "Terrific. You know what you want and you know exactly how to get it, right? There's no room in this scenario for friends. No, indeed. Just Cassie struggling to beat the odds, just Cassie so damned determined to prove a point that it doesn't matter that it could have been easier. What a martyr! You'll accomplish it all on your own and then you can sit around in lonely isolation and rejoice in it. Is that what you want?"

"No. What I wanted was a till-death-do-us-part marriage with a man I loved. When I said those vows, I meant them. I wanted my son to grow up knowing his father, instead of reading about him in the sports pages or on the cover of some supermarket rag. I didn't have big dreams, J.K. I didn't think I was asking a lot," she said, her eyes bright with unshed tears. "But life's not always fair. I am alone. Teddy doesn't have a father ninety-nine percent of the time. This is the hand I've been dealt and I'm doing the best I can to cope with it. If that makes me a martyr, so be it."

Her shimmering gaze blazed up at him. "The one thing I really don't need is you coming round constantly and telling me what I've accomplished is not enough."

J.K. felt as if she'd landed a solid blow with a bat. There was so much pain in her voice, but he couldn't miss the determination as well. She was going to make it and without his help, if she had her way. He sighed heavily and searched his brain for a compromise, one she'd accept.

"I'm sorry, Cassie," he said softly, wiping at the tear that trickled down her cheek. "I swear I never meant to make things worse for you. I don't know how to do this. I know I'm blundering but you gotta believe me, I just want to help."

She blinked back fresh tears. "Don't you think I know that? But I don't need your money, J.K. It just makes me feel more like a failure. Everybody warned me I was making a mistake marrying Ryan when we were both just kids. I was too stubborn to listen and I was wrong. I wasn't ready for marriage."

"Stop kicking yourself. Ryan wasn't ready, not you. You didn't fail. He did. Don't you understand that?"

"And now? Who's failing now, J.K.? There's no one around to put the blame on except me."

"Dammit, you're not a failure. You're just struggling to get on your feet. You'll make it, Cassie. You're tough. You'll get through this rough patch."

"Not if you keep trying to pick me up. I need to do it on my own, J.K. Don't you see? It's important to me to prove I can do it all on my own. The job I have now may not be much, but it's a first step. I got it without anyone's help. I'm good at it and I'm going to get better. Who knows, I may even go back and finish college. One of these days I'll actually have an identity of my own, instead of just being Ryan Miles's ex-wife. No matter how long it takes or what kind of sacrifice I have to make, I'm going to make something of my life. I'm going to be somebody."

"You are somebody, Cassie. Hell, Cassie Miles is the most special woman I've ever met."

"Not yet," she denied, her expression fiercely determined. "But I'm getting there."

For the first time, he began to understand her point of view and to accept her determination. "Okay," he relented finally and with great reluctance. "I won't try to interfere anymore. Just remember that I'll always be around to back you up. Think of me as an insurance policy."

Something about his words made her smile. "Insurance, huh? Couldn't you just be my friend, J.K.? That's what I need the most," she said softly. "I could really use a friend."

Without conscious thought, J.K.'s arms opened and Cassie moved into them. He felt her whole body shudder as he closed the embrace. "You have one, babe. You have one."

It wasn't exactly the role he'd had in mind, but it would do for now. It would do.

Tomorrow, however, would be a different story.

Six

Now that the ground rules had been spelled out, Cassie felt as if she could finally relax and just enjoy J.K.'s company. There would be no more subtle attempts to underwrite her expenses, no more pestering her to get into a legal battle with Ryan over money. There would definitely be no more unexpected, bone-melting kisses. That's the way she wanted it—the only way it could be—and J.K. had agreed.

Well, he'd agreed about the money, anyway. In retrospect, she wasn't so sure about the kisses. She carefully reconstructed the conversation in the supermarket parking lot and realized she might not have mentioned that ground rule as clearly as she should have. She had insisted that all she was looking for was a friend. That should imply no kissing, shouldn't it?

Probably not to a man as blatantly sexual as J.K., she admitted reluctantly. He'd looked very much like a man intent on kissing, even when they'd been in the middle of that face-off over the shopping cart. And as mad as she'd been, the idea had definitely crossed her mind, too. The man's appeal was impossible to ignore. He had a body like... Oh, brother! she thought, catching herself in midlust. She hoped she'd gotten that no-kissing point across, because obviously her traitorous hormones had other ideas.

Still, overall she was feeling pretty good about making herself heard, standing up for herself, not letting him ride roughshod over her. It would be all too easy, especially in her present circumstances, to give in and let a take-charge man like J.K. handle things. She hadn't done that.

She was so busy congratulating herself on her victory that she was stunned when the florist's delivery boy came waltzing into her office with a bouquet less than one week later. Fortunately, he looked as if he lifted weights in his spare time, because the awesome arrangement of colorful spring flowers he was carrying was just about the size of Texas.

Her co-workers, three blatantly curious nurses and the only slightly more restrained office manager, surrounded her desk before she could gather her wits. She grabbed the card, which was tucked amid the tulips, daffodils and irises, and hastily stuck it into her desk drawer.

"Aren't you going to look to see who they're from?" Ellen, the office manager, said.

"I know who they're from," she said with a little sigh of resignation. Why hadn't she thought to include flowers in the ground rules? She struggled to pick them up and move them to a credenza where they'd be out of the way and almost out of her sight. She didn't want to be reminded of exactly how persuasive J.K. could be once he set his mind to it. The man had been practicing seduction since the age of ten. He was bound to be a master at it by now. Sending lavish flower arrangements after an argument was probably second nature to him. Considering his bossy temperament, he probably kept a standing order at the florist's.

"Come on, Cassie, tell us," Jennifer Martin pleaded. "Are they from your ex?"

"Hardly."

"Then you have a new beau. How romantic!" She sighed. She was barely twenty-one and still thought romance came directly from the florist. Cassie wasn't quite ready to disabuse her of that notion. She figured reality would set in soon enough.

"No new beau," Cassie asserted. "They're from a friend."

"Some friend," said Mary Beth, casting another envious look at the spectacular arrangement. "I'm doing good if John picks up a bunch of carnations from the vendor on the corner for our anniversary."

"The size of the gesture is not necessarily indicative of the sincerity." Even as the words were tripping

WOW!

THE MOST GENEROUS
FREE OFFER EVER!
From the
Silhouette Reader Service™

GET 4 FREE BOOKS WORTH $10.00

Affix peel-off stickers to reply card

FOUR FREE BOOKS

4 · 4 · 4 · 4

FOUR FREE BOOKS

PLUS A FREE VICTORIAN PICTURE FRAME

AND A FREE MYSTERY GIFT!

NO COST! NO OBLIGATION TO BUY!
NO PURCHASE NECESSARY!

Because you're a reader of Silhouette romances, the publishers would like you to accept four brand-new Silhouette Desire® novels, with their compliments. Accepting this offer places you under no obligation to purchase any books, ever!

YOURS

We'd like to send you four free Silhouette novels, worth $10.00, to introduce you to the benefits of the Silhouette Reader Service™. We hope your free books will convince you to subscribe, but that's up to you. Accepting them places you under no obligation to buy anything, but we hope you'll want to continue your membership in the Reader Service.

So unless we hear from you, once a month we'll send you six additional Silhouette Desire® novels to read and enjoy. If you choose to keep them, you'll pay just $2.24* each—a saving of 26¢ off the cover price. And there is *no* charge for delivery. There are *no* hidden extras! You may cancel at any time, for any reason, just by sending us a note or a shipping statement marked "cancel" or by returning any shipment of books to us at our cost. Either way the free books and gifts are yours to keep!

ALSO FREE!
VICTORIAN PICTURE FRAME

This lovely Victorian pewter-finish miniature is perfect for displaying a treasured photograph—and it's yours *absolutely free*—when you accept our no-risk offer.

Perfect for a treasured Photograph

Plus a FREE mystery gift! follow instructions at right.

SILHOUETTE DESIRE® NOVELS
FREE!

 Silhouette Reader Service™

```
AFFIX
FOUR FREE BOOKS
STICKER HERE
```

YES, send me my four free books and gifts as explained on the opposite page. I have affixed my "free books" sticker above and my two "free gift" stickers below. I understand that accepting these books and gifts places me under no obligation ever to buy any books; I may cancel at anytime, for any reason, and the free books and gifts will be mine to keep!

225 CIS ACFL (U-SIL-D-02/91)

NAME
(PLEASE PRINT)

ADDRESS   APT.

CITY

STATE   ZIP

Offer limited to one per household and not valid to current Silhouette Desire® subscribers. All orders subject to approval.

```
AFFIX FREE
VICTORIAN
PICTURE
FRAME
STICKER HERE
```

```
AFFIX FREE
MYSTERY GIFT
STICKER HERE
```

PRINTED IN U.S.A.

WE EVEN PROVIDE FREE POSTAGE!

It costs you *nothing* to send for your free books — we've paid the postage on the attached reply card. And we'll pick up the postage on your shipment of free books and gifts, and also on any subsequent shipments of books, should you choose to become a subscriber. Unlike many book clubs, we charge *nothing* for postage and handling!

off her tongue, Cassie realized how stuffy she sounded.

"Come on, Cassie. Any guy who'd spend all that money must really care," Ellen contradicted.

"He's just spending what I save him on hamburger."

"Huh?" All four women stared at her in confusion.

"Never mind."

"You're really not going to tell us, are you?" Jennifer said.

"Sorry."

They sighed in collective disappointment and slowly returned to their own work, leaving Cassie to mull over the implications of J.K.'s latest tactic. She was still mulling—and reaching no conclusions she liked—when the door to the office swung open ten minutes before closing time. Looking tanned, virile and breathtakingly gorgeous, J.K. strolled in. His pleated gray slacks were straight from the pages of the latest men's fashion ads. His navy blazer was more traditional, but it hugged his shoulders in a way that would have made most men weep with envy. His shirt was pristine white and was offset by a daring pink-and-navy tie. Much as she wanted to, Cassie couldn't drag her eyes away from him. Her co-workers more than made up for her speechlessness.

"J.K. Starr!" Jennifer shrieked. "Oh, my God! Sandy, Ellen, Mary Beth get back out here. Midnight Starr is in the waiting room."

"Hey, sweetheart, how ya doing?" J.K. said, sweetening the drawled greeting with his famous grin.

Jennifer sank back in her chair. The other nurses stood in the doorways of their respective treatment rooms, mouths gaping. Ellen dashed out of the rest room so fast only her top lip had lipstick on it. Cassie shook her head at the display of female hormones screeching into overdrive.

Why was he doing this to her? First the supermarket. Now her office. Was there to be no place where she was safe from his determined assault on her senses? Why tonight and why, dear God, here? These women would never, ever let her forget it. There was little hope that J.K. had turned up by accident, unaware that she worked in this particular office. Nor was it likely he wanted to see one of her employers. They were pediatricians. Even so, she was tempted to ask if he had an appointment. Maybe that, with a pointed glance at the waiting room filled with toys, would reduce him to size. Before she could gather her wits, though, J.K. was hovering over her, an all-too-familiar glint of mischief in his eyes. He dropped a friendly kiss on her forehead to a chorus of background sighs.

"Damn," she said.

"Make that *hot damn* and I'll feel better."

She regarded him malevolently. "Don't press your luck. What the hell are you doing here? How did you even know where to find me?"

"Why are you cursing?" he evaded.

"The kissing," she moaned, whacking her forehead where only seconds before J.K.'s lips had been. "I knew I should have been more explicit about the kissing. No more, J.K." She shook her head, speaking firmly. He was laughing at her. Her gaze narrowed. "And don't laugh at me."

"Maybe you'd better write out all these rules. I remember the one about the money, but I'm getting confused about these new ones."

"You remember. You're just being stubborn and selective."

"Maybe so," he agreed cheerfully. He glanced at the flowers dominating the credenza. "I see you got the flowers."

"Yes, thank you," she said politely, refusing to meet the perfectly enthralled gazes of her co-workers. "They're lovely." She swallowed hard and tried not to notice that he was perched on the edge of her desk, his rock-solid thigh within inches of her fingertips. She would have told him to move, but the only other chairs nearby were built for five-year-olds. "Why are you here?"

"I thought maybe we could go to dinner. Take in a movie. How about it?"

She shook her head. "I can't. Teddy's waiting for me."

"Nope. Billy's mom said he could stay there tonight."

"He has school tomorrow. He can't spend the night with a friend."

"No school. A teacher planning day, I think."

"What do you know about teacher planning days?"

"I made it my business to know about this one. Even as we speak, the boys are working their way through a stack of the latest videos."

"Supplied by you, no doubt."

"I didn't want to leave anything to chance."

"You forgot one thing."

"What?"

"You're supposed to ask me before you go making all these arrangements for my life. That was definitely part of the deal we made. I remember specifically discussing that the very first time you came by."

"Could be, but I decided I prefer a sure bet. If I'd asked you first, you'd have made some excuse or other, just like you're doing now. This way I've already covered all the contingencies."

"Except one," she insisted. "I'm saying no."

Four women moaned in the background. J.K. winked at them.

"Don't be stubborn, Cass. I had a lousy day at the ballpark. I need someone to talk to."

If he meant to appeal to her kindness and understanding, he was off base. She was feeling about as understanding as Attila the Hun. "Go down to the Blue Dragon. I'm sure some of your teammates will be able to cheer you up."

He apparently didn't intend to give up that easily. "I don't want to talk about baseball. I need a woman's comfort."

She gestured grandly at the still-staring women behind her. "Take your pick. Except for Mary Beth. She's married."

"That's okay," Mary Beth said, wide-eyed. "I could make an exception."

"Sorry, ladies," J.K. said. "I've already made my choice."

He said it with such confidence, such sincerity. Cassie began to waver. She stared at the pile of medical records on her desk. She'd planned to have them all filed before she left for the night. Ellen caught the direction of her gaze and apparently guessed where her thoughts were headed. "Don't worry about the filing," she said. "Jennifer and I will finish up. You deserve a night on the town."

"Traitors," she muttered.

"See," J.K. said, ignoring her comment and grinning in satisfaction. "No more excuses."

He was right, she thought in resignation. She couldn't think of a single one. And there was this one movie she'd been dying to see, a romantic comedy. It was the sort of movie J.K. and Ryan had always hated. It would serve him right.

"I'll only go if I get to pick the movie," she said finally.

"You're on."

She managed a weak smile for her still-gaping friends. For some reason she didn't feel all that victorious. In fact, she felt as if she were walking into a deadly trap.

The restaurant only accented her fears. It was expensive and romantic. The maître d' greeted J.K. with deference and led them to a secluded table, lit by candlelight. The low, mellow music was provided by a pianist who could have performed for elevator recordings. Her menu had no prices and no entrées that she recognized. She glanced across at J.K. and felt her pulse begin to hammer to an unexpectedly sensual rhythm.

"You're not playing fair," she accused, deciding the best defense was a good offense. Would a baseball player understand that tactic or was it football? Or politics? Whatever, it didn't seem to be fazing J.K. He met her gaze evenly.

"Who's playing?" he asked.

"You are. First the flowers. Now this."

"I'm just treating you the way you deserve to be treated."

"No, you're treating me the way you would a lov—" She stammered to a halt, her face turning fiery.

"A lover," he said softly, leaning toward her. The candlelight made the blue in his eyes dance with invitation. "Is that what you were going to say?"

She nodded, captivated by that barely contained hint of aggression, the definite sizzle of passion. Even out of practice she recognized desire when it was sitting across from her. It made her very, very nervous, especially since it seemed to be striking some responsive chord deep inside her.

"That's how I see you, Cass."

"You promised, J.K.," she said, her voice weak with sudden longing. If only... She snapped herself back to reality. Old apprehensions made her cautious. Men like J.K. left women like her. She wasn't flashy enough or provocative enough to compete with all those women who waited willingly on the sidelines in every ballpark in the country. She wasn't Susan Sarandon in *Bull Durham*, witty and self-confident and looking for nothing more consequential than a short-term fling with a summertime hero.

"I'm just here as your friend, if that's all you want," J.K. reassured her. "I'm just hoping that sooner or later I can change your mind."

"Why? For the challenge of it? Those four women in my office, Mary Beth included, would have died to be sitting here with you tonight. Why me? It can only be because I'm the one saying no."

"You're not giving yourself enough credit. Now let's not debate this anymore. We're here because we both want to be here, whether you're ready to recognize the fact or not. Why don't I order for us both? Is that okay?"

"Please."

They'd finished the escargot, sampled the pâté and were well into the veal before Cassie finally relaxed and realized she was actually having a good time. It was like the old days, only Ryan wasn't there. This was just J.K., her pal. What harm could she come to with an old and dear friend?

Her guard was down by the time they arrived for the late show at the big multicinema mall. J.K. looked at the poster advertising her movie choice and faltered. To his credit, though, he didn't argue, didn't try to persuade her to switch to an action movie starting at the same time. He bought the tickets and, over her protests, the biggest container of buttered popcorn, two large sodas and a giant box of candy.

"J.K., we just ate a huge meal," Cassie said as he tried to juggle his purchases. She made a grab for the popcorn just as it tilted precariously.

"Force of habit. Movies require very specific sustenance. Can you get the door?"

She rolled her eyes and opened the door to the already-darkened theater. As soon as their eyes were accustomed to the shimmering light from the huge screen, J.K. led the way down the aisle and found two seats in the middle. Cassie was sure they were the same two seats in the same row he sat in every time he went into the theater. "Another habit," she murmured.

"Hmm?"

"Nothing."

A nearby chorus of hisses silenced them as the credits began to roll. The director's name hadn't even completely rolled up the screen before Cassie realized she might have made just the tiniest miscalculation. The emphasis in this particular comedy was clearly going to be on the romance. And the star looked a lot like J.K., whose knee was bumping hers and whose fingers kept grazing hers over the popcorn. She tugged at the collar of her dress. Where the heck was the air conditioning in this place? By the time J.K. draped his arm across the back of her seat, his hand resting lightly on her shoulder, Cassie felt as if she'd been sequestered in a steam room.

Midway through the first of what seemed destined to be a great many love scenes, J.K.'s fingertips brushed lightly along her nape. Sparks shot through her. Then he began a slow, sensual massage that made every bone in her body melt.

Science fiction, she thought desperately. She should have insisted on science fiction. Or maybe a techno-thriller. Then she wouldn't have understood what was happening, wouldn't have cared and would have drifted happily off to sleep. Asleep, she would not have noticed the effect of J.K.'s touch.

Wanna bet? Oh, hell, she thought, scrunching down in her seat in what turned out to be a futile attempt to escape J.K.'s provocative touch. Four love scenes later and after at least fifteen views of an incredibly tantalizing male posterior that resembled the shape of J.K.'s—or at least looked like J.K.'s in a bathing suit, she amended with all due modesty—Cassie was on fire. Her whole body hummed with awareness. J.K. leaned over to whisper in her ear and the sensation of his warm breath on her neck make her cling desperately to the armrest. She had no idea what he said. Fortunately, he didn't seem to expect a response. Or else he was content just to listen to her heavy breathing.

It doesn't mean anything, she told herself. It's habit, just like the popcorn and fruit-flavored candy.

It didn't feel like habit. It felt incredibly special.

Who was she kidding? It felt like danger. Wonderful and alluring, but dangerous nonetheless. She shivered as he whispered something more, then brushed an innocent kiss across her cheek.

Innocent, my Aunt Tilly! Nothing J.K. ever did was innocent, she lectured, trying to ignore the way her blood was pounding just as hard as if he'd meant it. He was still determined to seduce her and he was doing a damn fine job of it. One more love scene on screen and one more fleeting kiss by J.K.'s velvet-soft lips and she'd be ready to throw him down in the aisle and have her way with him, audience or not. The man ought to be declared a lethal weapon.

Cassie was on her feet, shaken but steady, the second the final credits began to roll. J.K. grabbed her hand and pulled her down. "I want to check out the cinematographer. He did a great job, don't you think? Especially on that shower scene. Pretty steamy stuff, huh?"

Steamy? They could have cooked broccoli in that shower. "I didn't notice," she said.

"Liar," he accused, grinning and still clinging to her hand. "I can feel your pulse racing just at the mention of it."

"Caffeine," she improvised. "We drank all that coffee at dinner and then the soda. It always makes my pulse race."

"Nice try, but we had decaf at dinner and the sodas were caffeine free."

"Oh." Even in the dim, flickering light, Cassie could see his smirk. She had to get away from that knowing look. It might be cowardly, but she'd never claimed to be anything more. "I think I'll go to the ladies' room. Meet you in the lobby," she said and hurriedly slid out of her seat before he could react.

In the rest room she dawdled. She splashed cool water on her face and then let it cascade over her wrists. It was meant to chill the white-hot sensations running riot through her, but it failed dismally.

"You are heading for disaster," she warned her wide-eyed reflection in the mirror.

"Cass?"

Her eyes flared even wider at the sound of J.K.'s hushed, anxious voice just outside the door.

"Cassie, are you still in there?"

She groaned.

"You can't hide forever, you know. They want to lock this place up before morning. They'll throw you out eventually."

She dried her hands and face and marched out, head held high. "What makes you think I was hiding out?"

He grinned. "Experience."

"Maybe I was just trying to make myself more beautiful for you before we went home. Isn't that what your dates usually do this time in the evening?"

Bad move, she thought as J.K.'s whole body visibly tensed at the unintentionally flirtatious remark. He stared at her with an intensity that was unnerving.

"Cass?" There was a sudden questioning look in his eyes. His voice hovered between vulnerable and hopeful. That tone almost did her in. She drew in a deep breath and steeled herself against it.

"I mean you go to your home and I go to mine," she said desperately. "Not the two of us together."

She watched the flare of passion being rekindled in his eyes and shook her head emphatically. "Oh, no! Forget it. You get that notion out of your head right this minute, J.K. Starr."

He nodded seriously, but there was the faintest suggestion of a smile playing about his lips. "Whatever you say, Cass. Whatever you say."

Seven

———

"**W**hatever you say."

That's exactly what J.K. had said to her. Cassie distinctly remembered not only the words but the precise context in which they'd been spoken. Apparently, however, she hadn't said nearly enough or maybe she'd said all the wrong things. At any rate, J.K. drove straight past her office and car and on toward her house at a breakneck pace. She knew there was something in politics called damage control, a quick fix when a misstatement caused seemingly irreparable harm to a campaign. She really, really needed a little damage control right now. Unfortunately, she had no idea how to bring it into play in this situation. She'd set something into motion back there at the movies and for the life of her she couldn't imagine how to stop it.

No, a persistent, self-confident little voice nagged. That voice obviously belonged to someone with a complete grip on her senses. Cassie hadn't been that controlled since the day J.K. had turned up in response to Teddy's call. Any two-year-old knew that decisively negative word. Why couldn't she get that one, firm syllable past her frozen lips?

Cassie wasn't sure she liked the answer that popped into her mind. She did, too, want to object. She wanted to stop this before it went any further. She knew she had to. Having a casual fling with J.K. might help her temporary hormone imbalance—which she'd only just recently noticed—but it would play havoc with her life. Sex, even the very best sex, didn't last forever and she'd be damned if she'd be the one being left behind next time. So, she would say no.

At the door.

J.K. had her out of the car and inside the house before she could say spit. She'd forgotten he had keys, forgotten that Ryan had given them to him so he could look out for things that time they'd taken a camping vacation in the mountains up in Georgia. She'd also forgotten he could move that fast. It was the one thing she should have remembered about any ballplayer. They were trained to have moves so quick that only a dead-on fastball could catch them between bases. Obviously they practiced those moves off the field and J.K. was at the head of the class.

As his mouth swooped down to cover hers with velvet demand, she realized the one thing she hadn't forgotten was the devastating power of his kisses. She remembered that in spine-tingling detail. And she melted into his embrace with a tiny sigh of resignation and a whole ton of reservations.

Any minute now, she would say no, she promised herself. Any second she would pull away, regain control of her senses and slug J.K. in his arrogant, presumptuous jaw.

Just not this second, she thought as his tongue slid over hers, setting off yet another riot of bone-melting sensations. Maybe not even this hour, she thought as his fingers found the curve of her breast, caressing the peak into pebble-hard sensitivity. A hand swept down the curve of her spine, then over her buttocks, tipping her firmly into his heat and hardness.

Maybe not tonight, she conceded breathlessly. Maybe just this once she would indulge in feeling sensual and feminine and loved. Even if it was make-believe. Even if it didn't last.

"Let me love you, Cassie. Please."

It was the plea for permission that flipped her heart over. Not the kisses. Not the blatantly sensual, impossible-to-resist touches. Not even the impressive evidence of his desire. Just "please," and she was undone.

She couldn't make herself say a word—not yes and definitely not no. Whatever was happening between her and J.K., she couldn't walk away from it. Not yet. She simply nodded and slid her arms around his neck. Her lips brushed over the sandpapery texture of his jaw, leaving them tingling and aware. Her tongue tasted, discovering the lingering lemon and cherry of candy.

J.K. pulled back, his fingers trembling hesitantly against her cheek as he searched her eyes. "No regrets, Cass. I don't want there to be any regrets."

"No regrets, my friend," she said, trusting him that there would be no need for any. The man who was her friend would see to that. The man who was about to become her lover might be incapable of long-term commitment, but he would never abandon her as a friend. Despite the obstacles she'd placed in his way, he'd proved that many times over in the past few weeks. He'd stuck it out. He would be beside her through thick and thin and there was a lot to be said for that. It was more than she'd had from the man who'd vowed before God to stay.

At the door to her room she hesitated. Ryan was the only man who'd ever crossed that threshold. She'd never expected to want another man as much. The implications left her weak. As if he sensed her mounting reservations, J.K.'s hand cupped her chin, his thumb stroking the bottom lip she'd been biting in that instant of gut-wrenching confusion and indecision.

"Any time, Cassie. You can stop this anytime you want to."

"No," she said now, when it had a different meaning entirely. "No. This is what I want. Promise me, though, that we won't try to pretend that it's anything more than what it is."

"Meaning?"

"Don't say you love me, J.K., and don't let me say it, either. The lie would cheapen it. This can be something special, just for what it is."

He opened his mouth, but she stood on tiptoe and sealed her lips over his, stopping the protest, changing the direction of his thoughts back to wicked, back to devil-may-care, back to loving. She didn't stop the kissing and the tasting until she was sure that only the heat flaring between them mattered anymore.

J.K. wondered how Cassie would react if he took her right where they were standing. His whole body trembled with the effort it took to keep from losing control. Her deep, wet kisses first startled, then delighted him. Now they were turning him into a quivering mass of needy male protoplasm. Make that a hardened mass. He was aching with his hunger for her. Her king-size bed, littered with her silly, charming collection of stuffed animals, seemed much too far away. If they didn't slow down, they'd never get there.

"Cass," he murmured, placing feathery little kisses along the column of her neck. He nibbled on her ear. "Slow down, babe. We have all the time in the world."

She murmured a protest as her fingers began working the buttons on his shirt. He clasped her hands and stilled them against his chest. A puzzled look crossed her face as she stared up at him. "Why?"

"Because I am about to toss you down on this floor and I don't want it to be that way. I've been hungry for you for too long now. I hurt all over."

Her hands slid down, tentatively grazing the front of his slacks. He groaned as a shudder swept through him. "You're playing with fire, Cassie."

She gazed up at him with a pert smile. "Oh, is that what you call it?"

He shook his head. "Why is it that I never suspected this cruel streak in you?"

"Cruel? I'm just giving you a dose of your own medicine."

Satisfaction surged through him. "So, it did get to you when I touched you in the movies."

"Don't feign innocence with me. You knew exactly what you were doing."

"Oh, I knew what I was doing. I just wasn't sure if it was working. You're a pretty tough customer."

"Just because I didn't swoon at your feet the first time you made a pass at me doesn't mean I wasn't aware of you. I just have a little more class than some women you've met."

"Honey, when it comes to class, you're the leader of the pack. Now that we've established that, why don't we try to find our place in this scene."

"You're calmer now?"

He nodded.

"Well, we can't have that," she said, reaching for him again. His shirt vanished and her lips found the masculine nipples buried in the thatch of dark blond hair on his chest. Every muscle in his body went taut. So much for slowing down.

"I think we'd better get into that bed, Cassie," he said, scooping her up and carrying her across the room. He shoved plush toys in every direction, then placed her squarely in the middle of the bed, her dress riding high on her thighs. He knelt at the foot of the bed and slipped off her shoes, then slid his hands slowly up one silky leg until he found the snaps of her garters. With a flick, he undid them and slowly rolled her stocking down, leaving a trail of searing kisses in the wake of cool, shimmery silk. By the time he'd repeated the process on her other leg, she was beginning to twist beneath him and her bare flesh was on fire.

"Help me with the dress, sweetheart," he whispered, kneeling now behind her and working on the zipper. Slow, lazy kisses burned down the column of her spine. When he was finished, she lifted the whisper of fabric over her head, turned slowly around and sat before him in lacy bra and bikini pants. He'd seen her before in no more. But quick, responsive heat swelled inside him as it never had before.

"Cassie," he began in a choked voice. He reached toward her, then hesitated. She was the one who completed the touch, taking his hand and placing it on her breast, then sighing with pleasure. "Love me, J.K.," she pleaded. "Hold me close."

As badly as he wanted to be sheathed inside her, he settled for simply taking her into his arms, savoring the sweet scent of her, delighting in her sensuous warmth and the promise of passion. How heavily would all this weigh on his conscience once tomorrow came, he wondered, then dismissed the thought. They were consenting adults. They were friends. They could handle being lovers without it changing anything essential between them.

It always changes things, his conscience warned. Always. But the temptation and the need were too great. Cassie was liquid fire in his embrace, drawing him as the eternal flame attracts the moth.

"This will be special, Cassie. I promise you that," he vowed as he slowly stroked and caressed until she cried out, coming apart beneath his touch, leaving herself vulnerable and unafraid. He stared into eyes shiny with tears and whispered, "There's more, sweetheart. Don't quit on me yet."

Her hips rose eagerly to meet his first slow thrust and her eyes widened with wonder. "That's it, sweetheart. Come to me." His whole body was alive with anticipation as each sure stroke took her higher and brought him closer and closer to a shattering climax in her arms. This waiting, this edge-of-the-precipice excitement was new to him. "That's it, babe. Let go for me."

"J.K.?" she murmured, part disbelief, part fear.

"It's okay. Go for it, Cass. All the way."

As shuddering contractions swept her along, he felt his own intense release wash endlessly through him until at last, filled with unmatchable joy and weak with exhaustion, he slept, Cassie in his arms.

He woke to find Cassie curled tight against his side, wide awake and intent on running her fingers through the hair on his chest.

"Did you sleep?" he asked groggily.

"Nope. I was too busy."

He opened one eye and encountered a glassy stare. He blinked and realized it belonged to an oversize panda. He heaved it aside and regarded Cassie intently. "Busy?"

"I had exploring to do," she said, her hand increasingly adventurous. J.K. moaned as desire rocketed through him again.

"What did you discover on this exploration of yours?"

"Oh, all sorts of interesting things," she said, pointing them out with magical fingers. J.K. had a feeling he'd unleashed a tiger. The thought was delightful and a little terrifying.

"Maybe we should talk," he suggested, drawing a sheet up and settling it over them. The suggestion met with blatant disobedience. "Cassie, that's not talking."

"Tell that to the phone company."

"Cassie!"

She grinned. "Do you really want me to behave, J.K.?"

"I really do," he said soberly.

"Oh."

Her disappointment was gratifying. His body agreed with her. After a fleeting wrestling match with his conscience, he gave in to the two of them.

Some time later, still damp with sweat and sleepily contented, Cassie murmured, "I do like the way you talk, Mr. Starr."

"You have quite a way with words yourself."

"J.K.," she began, then went silent.

"Hmm?"

"Why don't you ever talk about home?"

"Home? You've seen my house. What's to talk about?"

"Don't be deliberately obtuse. I'm talking about Kentucky and you know it. Why don't you ever say anything?"

The question whispered through the hairs on his chest and stirred a responding sigh deep inside him. He supposed she had the right to ask. Lying here in his arms gave her that right. But the question prodded like one of those pitchforks he'd used on never-ending bales of hay back on the farm.

"J.K.?" she repeated, then waited, endlessly patient.

"I suppose I just don't think about it much anymore. I haven't been back in a couple of years now."

"Don't you miss it? As much as I love Florida, I've never quite gotten over longing for the change of seasons in Wisconsin."

"You'd trade blue skies and palm trees for bitter winds and icy streets?"

"Not forever, but yes, I think I'd like to go back sometime. Since my parents moved down here, too, I haven't been back at all. I want Teddy to experience the way I grew up, the hot chocolate in front of the fire on Christmas Eve, making snow angels, skating on the pond down the road in winter and swimming there in summer. Didn't you ever do stuff like that?"

"Sure, but that's not what I remember when I think of home."

"What do you remember?"

"The loneliness," he said at once, startled to discover that the bitterness and anger of that time was still very much with him. He'd been so sure he'd

slammed the door tight enough so that he'd never have
to look back.

"But I thought you had a sister," she said, confusion in her eyes. "And I know you played ball. Surely
you had friends."

"I had friends."

"Then what? Tell me what was so rough."

"Who said it was rough?"

"You said it was lonely. Do you want to fight over
definitions?"

He sat up and the sheet fell to his waist. His movement dragged it off Cassie, leaving her bare chested
and vulnerable, but she didn't waste a second trying to
hide herself from him. She was too intent on her cross-
examination. The question made him uneasy. All the
probing, the hunt for intimacy nagged at him like a
burr. J.K. had never let anybody get close. He'd let
them into his bed often enough, but never into his
heart. Cassie was doing her damnedest to sneak onto
forbidden turf. She was trying to break her own fool
ground rule about not pretending this was anything
special between them.

"I have to go," he said, edging out of bed as his
defenses slid into place.

"If you leave now, don't ever come back." Her
voice was whisper soft, but deadly serious. He stared
at her. "I mean it, J.K. If we can't talk, then all
this..." She waved a hand over the bed in an all-
encompassing gesture. "It was a terrible mistake."

He stood there naked and feeling hideously vulnerable. The chill in her voice scared him as nothing else
had scared him in all his rough-and-tumble years.

"You've got a helluva way of getting to the heart of things, don't you, Cass?"

She smiled demurely. "I do try."

Only a man who'd watched her wrestle with demons in the past would have caught the flash of relief, would have noticed the tiny sigh. J.K. saw both and knew he couldn't walk away, no matter how badly he wanted to. She'd laid herself on the line getting into this bed with him. She'd compromised a lot of things she believed in, given herself to him wholeheartedly. The least he could do in return was tell her what she wanted to know. Talking about the past wouldn't kill him. Living it had made him tough enough to withstand almost anything—except the prospect of losing Cassie when he was just beginning to discover her.

"What do you want to know?"

"Everything."

"I don't suppose we could have this talk over breakfast."

She shook her head. "Nope. You'll talk faster if you have a goal of pancakes and eggs in mind."

"Lordy, but you're tough."

"It's something to remember," she said, her expression thoroughly satisfied.

He sat back down then, stretching out on the bed with his hands linked behind his head. The posture was relaxed enough, but his head was spinning with a kaleidoscope of painful memories. He sorted through until he found one simple, uncomplicated place to start: the farm.

He'd loved that farm. He'd even loved waking up at dawn to let the thoroughbred horses out into the fields. "Ah, Cass, you should see it sometime, especially at dawn when a gray mist hangs over everything. The bluegrass just goes on and on, rolling hill after rolling hill. There's nothing, *nothing* that smells quite like that earthy scent of fresh-cut grass, horse-flesh and morning mist."

She sighed and curled herself against him. "It sounds lovely. How can you not miss it? Are your parents still there?"

The tension, easing for a time, slammed back into him. "They're there," he said curtly.

"Didn't you get along?" she said, obviously sensing his turmoil.

"About as well as any kid gets along with his parents, I suppose."

She lifted herself up and studied him closely. "There's something you're not saying, isn't there? I can hear it in your voice."

He shook his head.

"J.K.?"

"It doesn't matter."

"Obviously it does. What was your father like?"

"He was a great guy. A little too absorbed with working the farm, but by all accounts a success and an all-round nice guy."

He sensed that Cassie was sifting through what he said, listening for nuances, searching for clues. Finding none, she said, "And your mother? Did she like living on a farm?"

His whole body froze with the ache of remembering. "Yeah, she liked it." He tried to keep his tone even, but Cassie clearly caught the bitterness.

"And?"

"And what?"

"There's more, J.K. Spit it out."

He thought back to that horrible, gut-wrenching day when he'd walked into the barn. His stomach turned over even now. "She was especially fond of the stable hands," he said finally.

Cassie sucked in her breath and then her arms went around him. "Oh, J.K., no," she whispered as she held him tight. Her compassion surrounded him, made the remembering a little easier.

"I'm afraid so, as I discovered rather vividly one sultry night. Near as I could tell, the whole town knew about her little habit, but they kept it under wraps out of respect for my dad. Funny, isn't it? Just when I realized how much he was respected by everyone, I lost all respect for him myself. He should have thrown her out."

"Obviously, he loved her very much."

"He was a fool."

He didn't realize he was crying until Cassie wiped away the dampness on his cheeks. He was so caught up in those awful emotions that he was hardly aware of her touch. "Quite a story, huh? Mr. and Mrs. Middle America. They deserved each other."

"Stop it," she said, her voice tender but impatient. "Apparently they'd made their peace with each other and it's not for you or me to judge them."

"Come off it, Cassie. Don't tell me you're not shocked."

"It doesn't matter what I feel. They had to live with it, not me."

"I had to live with it."

"No," she insisted. "You had to live with the way they treated you, and for all your bitterness I've never heard you say one thing to suggest that they didn't both love you, that they didn't do right by you. You grew up wanting for nothing. You got a good education. Some kids never have chances like that."

He'd never looked at his life from that perspective before. He supposed she had a point. That didn't make it any easier, though, to accept that his mother had been little better than a common whore.

"It does explain a lot, though," she said thoughtfully.

"What?"

"It's no wonder you've never settled down. You've convinced yourself that all women are untrustworthy, haven't you?"

"I've never given the matter any thought."

She tweaked the hairs on his chest, breaking the somber mood. "Maybe you should, big guy. You can do that while I fix the pancakes."

He didn't, though. He took a shower instead, dismissing Cassie's dime-store analysis. He was the way he was. What did it matter why?

When he walked into the kitchen, dressed in his slacks and the shirt he'd worn the night before with its sleeves rolled up, she gave him a questioning glance, but Teddy's presence saved him from the need to respond.

"Hi, Uncle Jake," Teddy said, accepting J.K.'s appearance readily. Fortunately he'd spent many a night in the guest room after those barbecues that had run on into the wee hours of the morning. It saved them all from an awkward moment.

"Are you here to take Mom to work? Is the car busted again?" Teddy wanted to know.

"Yes," Cassie said, clearly grabbing the easy explanation. "I had to leave it at work last night. J.K. said he'd drop by and take me in."

"I don't have school today," Teddy told him. "Maybe you could stay and play with me while Mom works."

"Sorry, pal. I have a game."

"Oh, wow! What time? Can I come?"

J.K. lifted his gaze to meet Cassie's. She was concentrating intently on her eggs. J.K. sighed. "I guess you'll have to work that out with your mother, slugger."

"Mom, can I go, please? You don't have to buy hot dogs or anything. I could probably even sit with Uncle Jake in the dugout, just like I used to with Dad. Please?"

J.K. watched the struggle on Cassie's face. "I'll think about it," she said finally.

"But, Mom..."

"I said I'd think about it, Teddy," she said sharply. "Now drop it."

Teddy's bottom lip went out. "May I be 'scused?" he mumbled.

"Yes," Cassie said. "Go."

Teddy gave J.K. a quick hug, then vanished. As soon as he was gone Cassie lifted a defiant gaze to J.K. "Go on and say it."

"Say what?"

"I blew it again, right?"

"I didn't say that. I do think you're making too big a deal about not letting him come to the ballpark. The guys adore him. He'd be out in the fresh air. There are a lot worse things he could be doing."

"Okay, okay. I will think about it. Did you consider what we talked about?"

"I was too busy thinking about last night. You were sensational, Cassie."

She battled against a smile and lost. "Thanks for the flattery, but it doesn't get you off the hook, J.K. You think I have all these unresolved feelings about Ryan that are standing in the way of my getting on with my life and that may be true. But you have just as many unresolved feelings about your mother. Promise me you'll give some thought to making peace with your parents. It might make a difference to your whole future."

He sighed heavily. "I'll think about it." He stood up and touched a brief kiss to her forehead, then realized he needed much more to get him through the day. His lips moved to her mouth for a slow, leisurely kiss.

"For good luck," he said, winking as he walked out the door.

"Yours or mine?"

"Maybe both."

Eight

Cassie's goodbye kiss had been potent. J.K.'s luck held through eight and two-thirds near-perfect innings. He had pitched a shutout so far, but now there were three men on base in the ninth and he was getting nervous. Still, he had two outs and he was two strikes up on Yankee first baseman Red Grady, a powerhouse hitter who couldn't seem to get a handle on his fastball today. One more strike and his team would have a shot at breaking the scoreless deadlock. After the way he'd pitched the other day, he needed this victory for his self-confidence.

It was the first time since the start of spring training that J.K. had gone the entire nine innings. He'd had to beg Ken to leave him in the game after the fifth, but he was tiring now and wondering if he hadn't made a serious mistake. His shoulder ached. He wanted the inning and the game to be over with in the worst way, but he'd be damned if he'd ask Ken to pull him with only one batter between him and that shut-out.

He watched for the sign from catcher Kyle Rogers, acknowledging it with the faintest suggestion of a nod. Never was he more aware of the tension in his muscles, the soft leather of his glove, the weight of the ball and the roughness of the stitching than at a turning point like this. He could feel the blazing afternoon sun beating down on his shoulders, the trickle of perspiration running down his back. Every sensation was gloriously magnified.

Grady shifted nervously at the plate, going through a familiar ritual. He took a few practice swings, tapped his bat on home plate, resettled his cap on his head and muttered something under his breath. He glared ferociously toward the pitcher's mound in an attempt to intimidate, but J.K. was long since onto him. Unlike other players who psyched themselves with threats and obscenities, Red Grady recited still-remembered chunks of his high school poetry assignments. The first catcher who'd mocked him for it had been eating dust five seconds later. That had taught J.K. an important lesson about body language and tone being every bit as important as content.

That's why he figured it was so much easier for him to see through Cassie's defensiveness. There was an underlying message every time they communicated and he doubted if she was even aware of it herself. Last night had been all the proof he'd ever need that he'd been reading her right all along. This, however, was no time to be thinking about Cassie, he reminded himself as he began his windup.

One more, Starr. One more strike and you're out of here. Let some other sucker pitch the extra innings if the guys can't pull it out in the bottom of the ninth.

The tension in the stadium was almost palpable. Even though it was only spring training, the fans took each exhibition game seriously. J.K. tried to make himself relax into the throw, but his fingers gripped the ball too hard. Sweat beaded on his brow and ran into his eyes, but he never once looked away from Grady. For him there was an intensity, an undercurrent of electric anticipation in that instant before a pitch that was unmatched by anything he'd ever experienced, except maybe great sex.

Grady stepped out of the batter's box in an attempt to break his concentration. J.K. turned his back on the plate, picked up his resin bag, dusted off his hands and wiped them on his uniform. When he turned back, Grady was in place and he was ready. J.K. brought the ball in to his chest, then out again. As he reached the peak of his pitching motion, an excited voice split the air.

"Uncle Jake! Hi, Uncle Jake!"

"Balk!" the umpire shouted as J.K.'s motion jerked to a stop in midwindup.

J.K. groaned. He couldn't even bring himself to look toward the dugout as the third-base runner sauntered home, putting the Yankees into the lead. He could hear Ken's furious stream of objections and could imagine the expression on his face. His own feelings were mixed. He almost never balked. He had a smooth pitching motion that rarely faltered. The fact that he had at such a critical point in the game was humiliating.

But knowing that Teddy was in the stands almost made it worth it. If he was there, then Cassie had brought him after work, which had to mean she was coming around. Maybe, at long last, she was putting things back into perspective. Maybe the fantastic lovemaking they'd shared last night had been a critical turning point in her recovery. The memory of the way she'd come apart for him was every bit as hot and disturbing as the afternoon sun.

Thoroughly distracted by Teddy's one innocent yell and all it implied, J.K. finished the inning in a daze. The Yankees scored twice more before he got the side out. Disgusted, he walked to the dugout and took a seat as far away from the furious manager and his teammates as he could. Ken would have plenty to say once they hit the locker room, but for now he was going to try to get them out of the last half inning with some pride.

"Sorry, guys," J.K. apologized after the game ended as their first loss of the still-young training season.

"Hey, J.K., it happens to the best," Kyle told him with a pat on the back.

"Sure, amigo," Davey said. "We take them next time. Come, have dinner with Maria and me. We'll drink a few beers. You'll forget all about it."

He thought of Cassie someplace nearby, waiting for him, he hoped, as she used to linger at the locker-room entrance waiting for Ryan. "I don't know, Davey. I might have a date tonight."

"Bring her. She can help Maria in the kitchen."

"Don't let her hear that sexist talk. She'll have you scrubbing pots and pans before the night is out. I'll talk to her and see what she wants to do. I'll give you a call if we're coming." His expression turned sober. "Thanks, pal."

Davey waved off his gratitude. "*Por nada.* We are friends, right? Besides, Maria has been complaining about missing you. I think she has a crush on you like all the others. You will watch your step with her, *si?*" There was a mock threat in his voice.

J.K. laughed at the thought of tangling with the feisty Maria. "Definitely *si*, my friend. Your wife is safe. She's too much woman for me."

The exchange with Davey improved J.K.'s mood, but Ken was less forgiving than his teammate. "In here," he hollered, when he spotted J.K., a towel draped around his hips, on his way to the showers. Anxious to get cleaned up, J.K. hovered in the doorway of the manager's dingy office. The place was such a mess it was rumored that a couple of his teammates had gotten lost in there and were never seen again. The bodies were probably under that stinking pile of towels in the corner.

"What the hell happened to you out there?" Ken demanded. "That was the sorriest excuse for pitching I've ever seen."

"Hey, lay off," he said defensively. "I had eight great innings."

"It takes nine to win a game."

"So why didn't you yank me after eight?"

Ken didn't even deign to answer that one, since they both knew perfectly well that it was J.K.'s own stubbornness that had kept him in the game. "Maybe there's a lesson in here, Starr."

"Maybe so."

His ready acknowledgment seemed to startle Ken. "Just think about it," the manager mumbled before waving him off.

"I'll do that," he agreed, hurrying off to shower so he could get back outside to see if Cassie was still around. His hair was still damp when he emerged from the locker room ten minutes later. Teddy was waiting for him right outside.

"Uncle Jake, you were great!"

J.K. scooped him up for a hug. "Thanks, slugger, but I blew it."

Teddy patted his shoulder sympathetically. "That's okay, Uncle Jake. You did real good till the end." He frowned. "I guess maybe it was me yelling that messed things up for you."

Startled that Teddy was that astute, he said, "What makes you say that?"

"That's what the man next to me said. He told me to shut up."

"Don't worry about it, pal. I get paid to pay attention to what I'm doing. If I foul up, it's nobody's fault but my own." His gaze searched the area, but he saw no sign of Cassie. "Where's your mom?"

"In the parking lot. She said she'd wait by the car."

"Let's go find her, then."

"Can I have a drink first? I'm really, really thirsty."

"Let's check with your mom. Maybe we can stop for hamburgers or something. I'm pretty hungry myself."

"Wow! That'd be great. Hey, mom," Teddy yelled, taking off across the parking lot. "Uncle Jake's gonna take us for hamburgers."

J.K. winced, wondering how she was going to react to that news. He'd hoped to broach the subject a little more diplomatically, then casually mention the invitation from Davey and Maria. He should have known that a seven-year-old understood nothing about tact and strategy. He followed Teddy's progress across the nearly empty parking lot until his gaze finally fell on Cassie. She was leaning against the side of her car, wearing white shorts and a bright pink T-shirt that was knotted at the waist. With an old baseball cap perched on her head and no makeup on, she looked to be about fifteen. She was staring down at the scuffed toes of her sneakers, but glanced up at Teddy's untimely announcement.

"Hi," J.K. said, suddenly feeling awkward after last night's intimacy.

"Hi," she responded warily.

"How was your day?"

"Okay. Everyone at work was full of questions about you."

"I'm sorry."

She regarded him skeptically. "Are you?"

He decided to change directions. "I'm glad you decided to come."

She nodded curtly. "Did you win?"

"Afraid not. You didn't come in?"

"No." She shook her head as if to ward off the very idea. "I couldn't."

J.K. nodded. "Maybe next time. I'm still glad you brought Teddy."

She shrugged. "He gets his persistence from his father and I was running out of excuses," she admitted wryly. "What's all this about hamburgers?"

"Teddy's thirsty and I'm starved. I suggested maybe we could stop someplace. Davey and Maria wanted us to drop by there. How about it?"

He watched her whole body tense up and knew what was coming. "You told Davey about us seeing each other?" she said uneasily.

"Not exactly. I just said I had plans. He told me to bring along anyone I wanted. Come on. You and Maria used to be great pals. She'll be thrilled to see you. I think she's getting very tired of being pregnant. She'd probably enjoy a little female company. Davey's about as sensitive as a steel practice bat."

"Come on, Mom. Let's go someplace. I'm really, really hungry, too."

"I'm sure you are," she said with a shake of her head. "It's been at least two hours since lunch."

"Wait'll he gets to be a teenager," J.K. warned, laughing.

Cassie groaned. "I know. I remember what Ryan was like. He'd clean out the refrigerator at his place, then come over to work on ours. My father said he was going to have to take a second job just to support Ryan's milk habit."

"And bread," J.K. recalled. "I ate at least three sandwiches for lunch and another two for a midafternoon snack. Our housekeeper finally said if I was going to consume an entire loaf of bread by myself every day then I could bloody well go to the store and get it. That lasted about a week, until she realized how much extra money it cost once I got near the doughnuts."

"That's disgusting. You men act like pigs and wind up with muscles. If I ate like that, I'd be a hundred and eighty pounds of flab."

"I'd love you anyway," he said nobly.

"It would serve you right if I put you to the test on that."

Teddy was gazing back and forth between the two of them. Finally disgusted, he grumbled, "Are we going to eat or not?"

J.K. looked at Cassie, who gave a resigned shrug. "I guess we are."

"At Davey's?"

She hesitated. "Why not. Just don't give them the wrong idea about us, J.K. You know how talk like that travels."

"And you don't want it getting down to Miami that you and I are seeing each other, right?"

"I don't want it getting out at all," she said, casting a meaningful look at Teddy, who was already heading for J.K.'s car.

"Let's ride in Uncle Jake's car. It's neater than ours."

"A World War Two jeep is in better shape than ours," Cassie commented dryly. "Maybe we ought to take both cars, though. It'll be simpler later."

The prompt defensive maneuver worried J.K. He studied her questioningly. "Are you sure you're okay?"

"Why wouldn't I be?"

"I mean about last night."

"It was no big deal, J.K. That's what we agreed."

"People agree to a lot of things and then find the rules tough to live with. That's why there are so many divorces." He touched her cheek gently. "Don't regret last night, Cass. It was special."

She closed her eyes and sighed. "I know, J.K. I guess that's why it scares me."

"We need to talk some more, I think. How about cutting the visit to Davey's short and then I'll swing by your place for a while."

She shook her head. "Let's play it by ear."

J.K. sensed that she was retreating and he wasn't sure what to do about it, especially with Teddy waiting anxiously in the back seat of the car. Alone, he would have known exactly how to reach her. In bed, they had instantaneously attained an almost perfect understanding. He settled now for squeezing her hand, trying to communicate without words that he knew exactly the qualms she must be having and that they would work them out.

Once they were on the road, J.K. used his car phone to call Davey and let him know they were coming. Teddy was fascinated by the cellular unit.

"Let me talk, Uncle Jake."

"Too late, kiddo. He's already hung up."

"Could I call Dad? I'll bet he doesn't have anything this awesome in his car."

J.K. glanced over at Cassie. Her mouth was set in a thin, disapproving line. "Maybe you can try your father later on," J.K. said. "He's probably out at the ballpark now, anyway."

Teddy heaved a disappointed sigh. "Oh, yeah, right. I forgot." He sank back in the seat. Glancing into the rearview mirror, J.K. saw that he was staring dejectedly out the window. "We'll try him after dinner, son. I promise."

"It doesn't matter," Teddy said stoically. "He never calls me."

J.K. bit back a stream of obscenities and vowed that he would call Ryan tonight himself. He'd track him down wherever he was and have a long heart-to-heart talk with him about parental responsibility.

Even with all the reminders of Ryan's faults and their impact on his son, J.K. realized he was feeling astonishingly contented being with Cassie and Teddy. If he didn't watch his step, he was going to find himself caught up in something he'd never expected when he'd first started spending time at Cassie's place. His goal had been to give her a little moral support. Then he'd developed a few immoral ideas and suddenly other wicked thoughts were creeping into his mind when he was with her.

Love. The word slipped into his head with all the sneakiness of a cat burglar. He could feel his stomach knotting at the very idea. *Whoa! Slow down, Starr. You don't even believe in love.*

But he did believe in Cassie and the warmth of their friendship. They were growing closer day by day. The sex was spectacular. And he adored Teddy. He guessed that was a form of love, just not the happily ever after kind, he reassured himself.

Whew!

"J.K., are you all right?" Cassie asked, her voice laced with concern.

He blinked and turned to her. He found that he had to fight the urge to slam on the brakes and kiss her right there in the middle of Dixie Highway with Teddy looking on. "Fine," he said in a choked voice.

She regarded him skeptically. "Are you sure? For a minute there you looked a little pale."

"Just hungry, I guess. Here's Davey's just ahead. I'll be terrific as soon as I get some food." He sounded far more confident than he felt. He had a feeling he wasn't likely to be fine until he could get his rampaging hormones and crazy thoughts under control.

He watched as Cassie swung her slender, tanned legs out of the car. Immediately his muscles tightened and heat blazed through him. So much for control. He abandoned the effort and stared, imagining his hands against the silken flesh, cupping that sweet little derriere, bringing her hips tight against his.

Holy mother of all the saints! He was definitely in trouble here. He gulped fresh air and thought of air conditioning and icy showers. The effect was only moderately successful. At least it would get him into Davey's without embarrassing all of them. Inside, with Cassie's legs discreetly under the table—please God, let Maria have a tablecloth on the picnic table—he might have a reasonable shot at getting himself under control. If he didn't, Davey and Maria wouldn't have to guess about the details of his relationship with Cassie.

Cassie approached Davey and Maria's front door as if she were being walked to the guillotine. This was the last place she wanted to be tonight, but she owed it to J.K. to make an effort to normalize her life. She'd been hiding too long and he was right—she had always liked the diminutive, fiery Maria. For all his machismo and bravado, Davey doted on his wife. Seeing them again would be okay, she reassured herself.

Maria swung open the door, a radiant smile on her face directed at J.K. Then she spotted Cassie. *"Mi amiga,"* she said, hurrying down the walk to throw her arms around Cassie. "You look *muy bonita.* J.K., why you not tell us you were bringing Cassie and the *nino?* Davey, hurry. Look who's here."

"Maria, it's so good to see you again," Cassie said sincerely. "How are you feeling? When's the baby due?"

"Yesterday, I wish," she said, grimacing. "I am very tired of this waiting. Come in. Come in. The others are on the patio."

Cassie hesitated. "Others?"

"Johnny and his new lady," she said with a meaningful lift of her expressive dark eyebrows. "Roberto and Anna. Kyle and Lauren. You know them all, except this new one. They will be so glad to see you, *amiga.*"

Teddy bounded up to Maria when he heard Roberto's name mentioned. "Is Joey here?"

"By the pool, *nino*. Go. He has missed you very much, I think. He has had only girls to play with for a long time now."

As Teddy took off around the side of the house, Cassie cast a desperate look at J.K. He put a reassuring hand on her shoulder. "It'll be okay, sweetheart."

She supposed if she had to confront Ryan's old gang again, she was glad to be doing it with J.K. at her side for support. In her heart she knew that they would be diplomatic. Ryan's name most likely wouldn't be mentioned. In fact, everyone would probably tiptoe around it until she felt like screaming.

"Come," Maria urged, apparently sensing her reservations. "You can help me in the kitchen for a minute. I am not so good at lifting these days."

Cassie smiled gratefully. "Of course. I'd be happy to help. J.K., you go on out."

He appeared torn, but he finally nodded. "I'll grab a soda for you and bring it in."

"That would be great and keep an eye on Teddy, please. I don't want him jumping into the pool with his clothes on," she said just as they heard a gigantic splash, followed by childish shrieks of laughter.

J.K. peeked out the door and grinned ruefully. "Too late. Don't worry, though. I think he did manage to get his shoes and socks off before he jumped."

"Terrific."

"There's still plenty of daylight left. He'll dry out in no time."

"I suppose," she said, silencing her worries. She was not going to start babying Teddy the way some divorced mothers did. This would not be the first time he'd been swimming in Davey and Maria's pool. It would just be the first time that Ryan wasn't around to watch him.

"I'll keep an eye on him," J.K. promised. "He's a good swimmer, Cass."

"I know that."

When J.K. had gone, she turned to Maria. "Now tell me, what can I do to help?"

"You can get that platter of hamburgers out of the refrigerator and take it to Davey, then come right back here and talk to me."

Cassie nodded, grabbed the heavy ceramic platter with its burden of burgers and took it outside. At the door she plastered a smile on her face and kept it there. She was greeted with friendly surprise and hugs from the wives. When she handed Davey the food and turned to go back in the other women trailed after her.

"You've been such a stranger, Cass," Anna said. "We've missed you."

"I've been busy. I'm working now and it seems as if there's never enough time in the day."

"Well, I'm glad J.K. was finally able to get you out of the house."

"He's been a good friend to Teddy and me."

"That's all?" Lauren said with blatant curiosity. "I thought I caught a little spark when he saw you come outside just now."

"An automatic response," Cassie said, feeling the heat rise in her cheeks at the lie. "J.K.'s eyes spark at the sight of any woman under the age of seventy."

"If you say so," Lauren said doubtfully.

"I know so. Now tell me what you all have been up to."

The conversation thus diverted and the first awkward meeting past, Cassie relaxed and enjoyed herself. J.K. was attentive without being obvious about it. She vowed to thank him later for his discretion.

It was only as the evening was winding down that all the careful subterfuge went for nought. Teddy was perched on J.K.'s lap, barely able to keep his eyes open.

"I think we'd better get this young man home," J.K. said.

"You're probably right."

"Are you going to stay at our house again tonight, Uncle Jake?" Teddy asked innocently, bringing the conversation on the patio to a screeching halt. No one said a word.

"Out of the mouths of babes," Lauren muttered under her breath.

"I'm ... we're ..." Cassie began, then floundered, hot pink color flooding her cheeks.

J.K. shrugged. "Cassie thought she heard a prowler last night. I went over to check it out for her."

The others nodded. The story was perfectly plausible. Clearly, however, not a one of them believed it.

"What prowler?" Teddy demanded, no doubt confirming that their skepticism was justified. "You didn't tell me about a prowler. I miss all the neat stuff."

Cassie turned to Maria and hugged her. "Thank you for everything. It really was good to see you again. If I can help when the baby's born, you call me."

"I will, *amiga*." She lowered her voice. "And do not let what the others think bother you. I think that you and J.K. would make a very good couple. He is, how do you say, more melted..."

"Mellow," Cassie corrected, grinning.

"*Si*, more mellow around you. And you have the light in your eyes again. That is very good."

"Thank you."

Once they were in the car, Teddy fell asleep at once. Cassie stared out the window.

"Cass," J.K. ventured, his voice tentative.

"Hmm?"

"You aren't upset, are you?"

"What would be the point," she said with a little sigh of resignation.

"It's true, you know."

"What?"

"What Maria said. I am more mellow since I've been with you and you do have a light in your eyes again. Let's not throw that away."

She turned and saw that his expression was grave. "Are you so sure we're not just deluding ourselves?"

"I'm not so sure of anything anymore. You seem to be turning my life upside down."

"And you think that's good?"

He reached for her hand, caressing her knuckles with the callused pad of his thumb. "I think that's very good. Let me stay tonight and prove it."

Desire spread slowly through her, just as he'd meant it to. "No," she whispered, her voice husky. "Not with Teddy in the house."

"When?"

"I don't know, J.K. If it's meant to be, we'll find a way."

"You're relegating me to cold showers?" he grumbled, but there was an amused twinkle in his eyes.

"You have other options."

His gaze caught hers and held. "No, Cass. As long as we're together, you're the only woman in my life."

The only woman in my life. The words sang in her heart, only to shatter a moment later when she remembered how they'd been prefaced: *As long as we're together.*

How long, she wondered. How long before he would tire of her? How long before some other woman would arouse his curiosity and stir his desire?

"Cass?"

"What?"

"We'll be playing out of town tomorrow and Sunday, but I'll be back late Sunday night. I'll call, okay? Maybe we could spend the whole day together on Monday. Teddy'll be in school, right? Could you get the day off?"

A whole day to be with J.K., to be held in his arms, to feel his touch again. It would be magic. Who knew how long it might have to last her. She nodded. "I suppose I could call in."

"Would you like to spend the day with me?"

How long? The question echoed. *You have now. Take it, Cass. Grab it and hold on.*

She lifted her gaze to meet his. "Yes, J.K.," she said, bold longing overcoming hesitance. "Yes, I'd like that very much."

He nodded, looking pleased. "Then I'll be by early."

At the door, with Teddy safely upstairs in his room, J.K.'s lips met her in a tender, fleeting caress that inflamed every bit as cleverly as the deep, hungry kisses they'd shared the night before.

"Very early," he amended.

Nine

J.K. made a point of calling Cassie from Clearwater on Saturday and again the minute he got back to town on Sunday night. It was the first away series the team had played since they'd been seeing each other and he suspected it would arouse all sorts of uncertainties for her. Besides, he admitted reluctantly, he missed the sound of her voice.

"Hi, sleepyhead," he murmured when she answered. "Sorry to call so late, but we just got back. I missed you."

"Did you win?" she asked groggily, stirring all sorts of memories. Waking up with Cassie could definitely turn out to be addictive, he thought as his body began to respond to her sleepy, sensual tone.

"We trounced 'em, nine to two."

"Did you have to pitch?" she asked.

"Nope. I sat around the bullpen wishing I were back here with you. What did you do today?"

"Cleaning, laundry, the usual chores. Teddy and I went to the mall for ice cream."

"A banana split?" he asked, remembering the last time and that instant when he'd first become shockingly aware of.Cassie as a desirable woman.

"Nope, just a cone."

The thought of her tongue slowly licking a cone of soft, melting ice cream made J.K.'s entire body ache. "Cass, don't do this to me," he pleaded.

"Do what?" Her voice was filled with innocence.

"You're teasing me," he accused.

"Not me. I'm too sleepy to tease."

"Maybe I should let you go back to sleep again, then."

"I suppose so," she said without conviction.

"Do you still want me to come over in the morning?"

"Yes," she said with far more enthusiasm. The yearning in her voice set his blood on fire.

"I'll call first," he promised. "Good night, Cassie."

"Night."

The phone was almost back in the cradle when he heard her call out his name.

"What, babe?"

"I missed you, too."

That sweet, breathless declaration kept him up the rest of the night. At six in the morning he went out for coffee and picked up a bag of doughnuts. At seven he was pulling up in front of her house. He walked around to the kitchen door, hoping to find Cassie awake and alone.

She was awake, but to J.K.'s shock she definitely wasn't alone.

The sight of Ryan Miles standing in the doorway to the kitchen with his arm draped possessively around Cassie's pajama-clad shoulders was like a blow to J.K.'s midsection. Ryan was doing all the talking, his expression intense. Cassie seemed to be clinging to his every word.

Damn! J.K. thought furiously. His friend's arrival today wasn't totally unexpected. He'd known since the beginning of spring training that Ryan's team would be heading into town on this date for a night game. He'd even looked forward to getting together over a few beers, trading a few insults and telling a few tall stories the way they used to when they shared a room on the road before Ryan was traded.

That, however, was all before Cassie became so much a part of his life. Finding Ryan here at the crack of dawn was the last thing he'd anticipated when he'd walked around the corner of the house. What kind of game was the man trying to play with Cassie's head now? She'd come a long way over the past few weeks. Friday night at Davey's had been a major hurdle, but she'd gotten over it. Even Teddy seemed to be feeling more secure. J.K. didn't want to see them hurt again, if this was just another of Ryan's thoughtless games. He assured himself that the sick feeling in his gut was sheer protectiveness, nothing more.

"And I'm destined for sainthood," he muttered in self-disgust as he paced the driveway trying to decide whether to go or stay. "Admit it, man, you're hung up on the woman and you're scared witless that she's going to dump you and go running straight back to Ryan."

He wasn't sure which astonished him more, the sudden awareness of the depth of his feelings for Cassie or his lack of self-confidence. Both were firsts. He'd never been attached to any woman so deeply that it had mattered whether she stayed or went. He'd always known he could walk across a ball field and pick just about any replacement he liked from the women in the bleachers. Right this minute, though, he didn't care about a replacement. He didn't care about anything but this newly discovered caring for Cassie and the whisper of fear that he could lose her.

Taking a deep breath, he tapped on the screen door, then opened it and walked in. Cassie's startled gaze collided with his. She looked guilty, which only accelerated the racing of his pulse. What would she have to feel guilty about unless Ryan was getting to her?

"So, buddy, how're you doing?" he said with forced cheer, dragging his attention from Cassie to the blond giant at her side. A familiar easy smile broke across Ryan's face as J.K. came through the kitchen into the living-room, dining-room area just beyond.

"J.K., what the devil are you doing here at this hour? I didn't think you ever got up before noon."

"I, umm, I thought I'd drop these doughnuts by for Teddy's breakfast. He hasn't left for school yet, has he, Cass?"

She shook her head, looking thoroughly uncomfortable.

"So, J.K., I hear you had a tough game against the Yankees the other day. The baseball writer in Miami did a piece on it. He said Ken had just pulled you in the second inning a few days before that. He wondered if you were losing your edge. You know how these jokers are. One or two bad days and they make a federal case out of it, you know what I mean?"

"Yeah," J.K. said. "That guy in Ohio wrote me off three weeks into the season last year. If he'd seen me in the ninth on Saturday, he'd be writing up my professional obituary."

"Don't worry about it, pal. You're bound to be a shoo-in for MVP again, maybe even the Cy Young Award. You've got a few more great years left in that arm of yours."

J.K. shook his head, puzzled by Ryan's too-jovial attitude. "Hey, the end of season's a long way off. I just worry about one pitch at a time," he said, snatching the cliché out of the repertoire he saved for interviews.

Ryan's arm slid down and settled around Cassie's waist. He squeezed and J.K.'s blood pressure rose. "Spoken with true humility, right, Cassie? Is this guy the greatest or what?"

J.K. watched as Cassie tried to extricate herself from Ryan's casual embrace. She refused to look at either of them.

"Would you like some coffee? I just made a fresh pot. I'll go get it." She took off for the kitchen before either of them had a chance to respond.

"What's bugging her?" Ryan said, staring after her. He shrugged. "Oh, well, you know women. Never will understand them. So, sit down here and tell me what's been happening with you."

J.K. bristled at Ryan's assumption that he was still the man of the house with the perfect right to issue invitations and play host. For one immature instant he wanted very badly to stake his own claim, but the image of Cassie's disapproval and possible embarrassment stopped him. It was obvious she found the whole situation awkward. The last thing she needed was two grown men having a territorial dispute in her living room. She'd probably toss them both out on their ears, just to prove exactly who was really in charge. Instead, he asked, "Have you seen Teddy yet?"

"No. He's still asleep. I told Cassie not to wake him, so she and I could have a little time alone."

"What for?" J.K. asked bluntly.

"Hey, man, what do you think? She's my wife."

"Your ex-wife," J.K. corrected, barely keeping his temper in check.

"Hey, what's bugging you?"

"Nothing. I just don't think you've got any right to come in here and play games with her head."

"Who's playing games? You know how I feel about Cass."

"No, I don't. How do you feel?"

"She's the greatest."

"Then why'd you divorce her?"

Ryan's gaze narrowed. "You're acting weird, you know that? If I didn't know better, I'd say you had the hots for my wife."

J.K. felt every muscle in his body go tense. "Don't be crude, Ryan. That's Cassie you're talking about."

"No. I was talking about you. Have you suddenly decided to do your playing around a little closer to home?"

J.K. rose to his feet with murder in his eyes. Fortunately, Cassie came back just then with the pot of coffee. The color in her cheeks told him she'd overheard every word. For her sake and her sake only, he backed off.

"Did Teddy know you'd be here this morning?" he said, shifting to more neutral turf.

"No. I thought I'd surprise him."

Which meant, J.K. thought uncharitably, that he hadn't been sure he'd be willing to leave his date in time to stop by. Before he could say anything to that effect, Cassie jumped in with an offer to go and wake Teddy.

"Why don't you let Ryan go?" J.K. suggested. "It'll be more of a surprise that way."

Ryan appeared startled by the suggestion. "Sure. That's a great idea. I'll be back in a few minutes."

Cassie sat down across from J.K. and began fiddling nervously with a napkin.

"What's wrong, Cassie?"

"What do you think is wrong?" she snapped. "Ryan shows up here out of the blue, practically in the middle of the night. He's acting like everything's perfectly normal. How do you expect me to react?"

"Are you glad to see him?" he probed.

Her gaze shot up and bright pink spots appeared on her cheeks. "Why would you ask anything crazy like that? Of course I'm not glad to see him. If it weren't for Teddy, I wouldn't care if I never saw him again.''

"Then why can't you look me in the eye?''

"Because...''

"Because why?''

"It just feels weird, that's all. The man had the nerve to walk in here and make a pass at me. Do you believe it?''

J.K. believed it so readily he felt like slamming his fist down Ryan's throat.

"It's been months since he's been around,'' Cassie went on. "He got the damned divorce he wanted and he thinks I'll still fall into bed with him whenever it's convenient.''

Which explained the tension he'd noticed when he first walked in. Ryan's overtures had apparently clashed head-on with Cassie's newfound sense of independence. He might have gloated if he hadn't been more inclined to go after Ryan and wipe up the sidewalk with that famed posterior of his.

"You have every right to be mad, Cassie, but what does that have to do with me? You're acting as if I'm at fault here, too.''

"I guess I am,'' she agreed. "You and Ryan, you were always such great pals. Listening to him this morning, watching him make his predictable moves just as if I were one of the bimbos he'd met on the road reminded me of everything I went through when we were married. He'll never change, not as long as he's wearing that uniform.''

"And you think I won't, either?''

Her chin rose defiantly. "Well, will you? Can a leopard ever change his spots? Ryan certainly hasn't."

"I'm not Ryan. You've seen the change in me yourself, Cassie. Hell, you're responsible for it. The last few weeks I haven't looked at another woman."

The declaration drew a faint smile. "A few weeks, J.K. That's hardly a glowing testimonial. Am I supposed to risk my whole future because you've managed to be faithful for the first couple of weeks of spring training? What happens once the team goes north?"

"I don't know," he admitted honestly. "What I'm feeling for you is still pretty new to me. I don't know how I'm going to react over the long haul. Does anyone?"

"Maybe not, but the odds are better for some than others. I think you definitely fall into the high-risk category."

"What do you want to do about that?" he asked, filled with tension. Ryan's arrival couldn't have been more ill timed. The fragile faith she was beginning to have in him was too easily shattered. Ryan had done it in a heartbeat.

"I don't know," she said miserably. "The only thing I want right now is to get through the next twenty-four hours with a minimum of damage to Teddy. Seeing his father always upsets him. How the hell is a seven-year-old supposed to understand a daddy who fits him into his schedule for one morning a year?"

J.K. shook his head. "If you and I can't understand it, we can't expect Teddy to. All we can do is to be here for him and make him realize that it has nothing to do with him, that Ryan just can't be any other way."

"So we excuse him?"

"Will it do any good not to? Is he likely to change just because we point out his flaws?"

"No, though God knows I've tried."

"Then let's just make the best of it and see that Teddy has a wonderful time with his father."

"You won't mind?"

"I can't say I'm crazy about it," he admitted, "but I'll live with it for Teddy's sake."

She lifted eyes shining with tears to meet his. "There are times, J.K. Starr, when I think you're very special."

"Hang on to those thoughts, sweetheart. I'm doing my damnedest." He held out his arms and Cassie moved into them for a quick, nervous hug. She was close one instant and back across the room the next. At his questioning look, she shrugged apologetically. "I told you, it feels weird with Ryan around."

"Cassie, he's clear back in Teddy's room. Besides, he's going to hear about us soon enough. We were at Davey's together the other night. If he and Maria don't talk, one of the other guys will."

"I know."

"Are you worried about how he's going to react?"

"I suppose."

Something inside him froze at her evasiveness. "Or is it that you're worried he won't react at all?"

"What is that supposed to mean?"

"Maybe I'm the one in the way here. Would you go back to Ryan if I weren't in the picture?"

"Absolutely not."

He listened for a false note, but there didn't seem to be one. "Cass, have you talked to him about the money?"

She bit her lip and shook her head.

"Why not?"

"I couldn't face the thought of a fight right off the bat."

"Let me talk to him."

"No. We agreed you wouldn't fight my battles for me, remember?"

"I don't mind."

"I do."

They were still at a standoff when Ryan and Teddy came in. Teddy was chattering a mile a minute. "And then I yelled at Uncle Jake and he... What was it you did, Uncle Jake?"

"I balked."

"Yeah, and the runner came in and scored and everybody was really mad. That man, Mr. Hodges, he came running onto the field and he yelled at the umpire, but it didn't help. We lost the game anyway."

"I see," Ryan said, studying Cassie thoughtfully during his son's recitation. J.K. watched the speculative gleam form in his friend's eyes. "I'm glad you're still getting out to the ballpark. Have you been playing ball yourself?"

"Mom plays catch with me sometimes, but she's not very good. Sorry, Mom. Uncle Jake's helped a lot, though."

"I see," Ryan said again, turning his gaze on J.K. quietly, "Thanks for taking such good care of my family, old buddy."

J.K. opened his mouth to respond, but Cassie said quietly, "We're not your family anymore, Ryan. J.K.'s been a good friend, but I take care of Teddy. We do okay."

"No thanks to you," J.K. muttered without thinking.

Ryan shot a questioning look at him.

"Maybe we'd better have a talk," J.K. said, refusing to face Cassie. He knew she was going to be furious.

Her hand clamped down on his arm. He looked at the nails biting into his flesh, then up into her warning expression. "Sorry, babe. I can't leave things the way they are. It's about time..."

"Don't do it, J.K.," she pleaded.

Ryan took the matter out of his hands. "I think maybe you're right, buddy. You and I seem to be long overdue for a talk."

Teddy watched the two of them anxiously. "Daddy, you and Uncle Jake aren't going to fight, are you? I thought you were best friends."

Ryan looked as if he were suddenly itching for a good brawl, but J.K. squeezed Teddy's shoulder reassuringly. "Nope, we're not going to fight. We're just going to talk. I promise. Your dad will be back inside in no time."

Cassie looked as if she wanted to strangle both of them. Instead, she said in a voice tight with strain.

"Teddy, if you want your father to take you to school today, you'd better hurry and get ready."

His eyes widened with excitement. "You mean it?"

She nodded.

"Yippee!" He took off at a run.

"Okay," she said, staring at J.K. "If you want to talk, do it in here."

"I think it would be best if we did this outside," J.K. said.

Ryan nodded his agreement. "It's between us, Cassie."

"Do either of you intend to bring my name into this private, all-male conversation?"

"Well..." J.K. squirmed uncomfortably.

"Hon..."

"I am not your *hon* anymore, Ryan Miles. I am your ex-wife," she said flatly before turning on J.K. "As for you, I've made it perfectly clear on more than one occasion that I don't want you interfering in my life."

"I think I have the right."

"No," she said emphatically. "You have no rights where I'm concerned. None!"

"Then what the hell was the other night all about?"

"What happened the other night?" Ryan demanded, his face flushing.

"Nothing," Cassie and J.K. said in unison, then stared at each other.

"Well, at least we agree about that," she said wryly. "J.K., I think you ought to go now."

"Not until Ryan and I have talked."

"Is this some sort of macho game with you? I told you to drop it."

"Okay. If that's the way you really want it, I'm out of here. Don't expect me to come running back, either."

"What the hell are you two talking about?" Ryan asked. "I feel as if I walked into one of those damned foreign films and found out they left the subtitles off."

"I know exactly what you mean," J.K. said. "Cassie's a hard woman to understand."

"Cass?" Ryan said, looking bemused. "There's nothing complicated about her."

"Maybe it just takes more practice than I've had yet. See you two at the ballpark."

J.K. got in his car, drove straight to the ballpark and walked into the weight room. Maybe if he spent the next few hours lifting weights he'd be too exhausted to punch Ryan out when he saw him with Cassie again tonight. And he had no doubts at all that Cassie would be there with Ryan. He'd practically forced her straight back into the man's arms.

There was a hard knot in J.K.'s gut all during the game against the Orioles. The anger ate away at him as he sat idly in the bullpen just thinking about Cassie and Ryan together. He watched Ryan's moves on the field, as smooth as ever, and couldn't help thinking that the man was just as smooth off the field, too. If he decided he wanted Cassie back, he'd talk her into it. J.K. had heard Ryan's line often enough. He knew just how persuasive he was capable of being.

And he had Teddy on his side. Cassie would do just about anything to make her son happy.

Including going back to an ex-husband who'd cheated on her, a man who'd repeatedly humiliated her? Come off it, Starr! Don't be a fool!

No matter how often he told himself that's just what he was being—a jealous jerk—he couldn't help feeling that Cassie was slipping away from him and heading straight for trouble.

It didn't help that he exited the locker room just in time to see Cassie, Teddy and Ryan getting into Ryan's car. Davey saw them, as well.

"I think we should go get a beer, amigo," he suggested, his dark brown eyes filled with sympathy.

"Good idea," J.K. said, slinging his jacket over his shoulder. "I think that's a damned good idea."

"Ryan is your friend?" Davey asked later, after they'd downed the first cold draft.

J.K. shrugged. "I thought so. I guess I never paid much attention to the way he was, you know what I mean?"

"He is not so reliable when it comes to women. Is that what worries you?"

"What worries me is that he's going to hurt Cassie again."

"Then tell her so. Warn her. Isn't that what a friend would do?"

"A friend, yes."

"But you want to be more than that," Davey said, astutely. "You think she will confuse your intentions?"

"I think she'll tell me to mind my own business."

"Is that so bad, if you think she needs to hear what you have to say?"

"No," he said thoughtfully. "You are right, my friend. You are very right. It doesn't matter if she gets mad at me, as long as she listens to what I have to say."

Unfortunately, the six beers it took for him to reach this momentous decision did nothing to enhance his equilibrium or his coherence. He stumbled up the front walk, leaned against the doorbell and waited for Cassie. She opened the door wearing a nightgown and a belted robe. She looked sleepy and flushed and infinitely desirable. She also seemed to be slightly irritated at being awakened. Not a good sign, he decided fuzzily. Definitely not a good sign.

"It is three o'clock in the morning," she observed. "What are you doing here?"

"I came to tell you..." he began, then lost his train of thought as he stared at the deep V of flesh where her robe was falling down. "I came to tell you that you are very beautiful." His voice was husky, but he thought fairly sincere.

She scowled, clearly exasperated, and tugged the gaping robe closed. "Thank you, but couldn't that message have waited until morning?"

"No. It's very important that I..." He swayed. "Whoops!"

She gave a heavy sigh of exasperation. "Get in here, J.K. I'll get you a blanket."

"I'm not here to sleep, Cassie. My sweet Cassie. Talk. We have to talk."

"Later, when you're making sense," she said curtly. J.K. stood in the doorway, still weaving unsteadily, while Cassie disappeared down the hall. She came back with a blanket and a pillow, tossed them onto the sofa and pointed. "Sleep it off, J.K."

"Could I have a little kiss?"

"Not in this lifetime," she said and vanished.

Too bad, he thought as he sat on the edge of the sofa and tried to master his shoelaces. They seemed to be beyond him, so he just tugged the shoes off and grabbed a corner of the blanket. It seemed to be stuck under him. He gave up and rolled over.

The last thought that flitted through his muddled brain was that Cassie was going to be mad as hell in the morning. And that he might very well deserve her wrath.

Ten

J.K. felt as if the entire percussion section of the local symphony orchestra was playing in his head.

Thrum! Loudly.

Thrum! Thrum! Thrum! Relentlessly.

Dragging himself to his feet, he staggered into Cassie's tiny guest bathroom and splashed cold water on his face. One glance in the mirror told him all he wanted to know about just how stupid he'd been last night. He'd been hoping it had been a bad dream.

Dammit all! Why had he allowed it to get to him? Why had it mattered so much that Cassie had left the ballpark with Ryan? What right did he have to come charging in here, loaded with more beer than sense, and warn her that she was making the biggest mistake of her life? Which she was, of course, but it wasn't any of his business if she was fool enough to give Ryan Miles a second chance.

The only positive thing he could recall about his foolish display of righteous anger was that Ryan apparently hadn't been around to witness it. Even in his drunken state, he'd taken heart from the fact that Cassie apparently hadn't let Ryan spend the night. Maybe this morning, after a gallon or so of coffee, he could calmly and rationally talk some sense into her.

If she was still speaking to him. The fact that she'd let him sleep on her living-room sofa wasn't exactly a promise of forgiveness. Quite the contrary in fact, considering where he'd slept the last time he'd spent the night in this house. All it proved was that even mad as hell, Cassie was too tenderhearted and too sensible to put him back behind the wheel of a car in the condition he'd been in last night. Today might be an altogether different story. Today she'd probably have his hide and take pleasure in every punishing second of it.

With that prospect facing him and those blasted drummers drumming in his head, he headed into the kitchen for coffee. While he waited for it to perk, he slumped down at the kitchen table, head in hands. It was several minutes before he realized he wasn't alone. It was the press of Teddy's body into his side that finally registered. He turned his head to find the boy studying him sympathetically.

"You and Mom had a fight last night, huh?"

"What makes you say that?"

"I heard you. She made you sleep on the sofa."

J.K. nodded.

"She used to make Dad do that, too. You want some breakfast? I can fix cereal."

The very thought of all those little, healthy flakes floating in milk turned J.K.'s stomach. "No, thanks, sport. Maybe later."

"I think what your Uncle Jake really wants is some humble pie," a voice said from the doorway.

J.K. listened hard for any evidence of amusement, but Cassie's tone was absolutely even. No humor. No anger. No feeling at all. It was worse than he thought.

"Teddy, why don't you get your cereal and take it into the family room," she said. "Aren't your favorite cartoons on this morning? You can watch until it's time to get ready for school."

"I'd rather stay here with you and Uncle Jake."

"Not this morning."

Teddy must have heard the soft but indisputable thread of warning in her voice. He fixed his breakfast and left without another word. Cassie poured two big mugs of coffee, silently passed one to J.K. and went to work at the stove. In no time the kitchen was filled with the greasy scent of bacon frying.

"You're trying to get even with me, aren't you?" J.K. said suspiciously, gesturing toward the frying pan. The aroma made his stomach turn.

"Why would I do that?"

"Because I behaved like an idiot last night."

"You'll get no argument from me about that."

"Would it help it I told you I was sorry?"

"It would help more if you explained why you felt it necessary to get drunk as a skunk and come charging over here like Sir Lancelot. My honor was never endangered, J.K.''

"I'm not so sure about that. I didn't like what I saw here yesterday.''

"What exactly did you see?''

"Ryan putting the moves on you. You even admitted he'd made a pass.''

She waved a spatula at him dismissively. "I am perfectly capable of handling Ryan.''

"Not if you're still in love with him.''

"Who said I was still in love with him?''

J.K. studied her closely. "You're not?'' he said doubtfully.

"Definitely not,'' she said and went back to stirring pancake batter. A minute later she was humming cheerfully. Any second now she was going to burst into off-key song and J.K. wasn't at all sure his pounding heart could take it. He decided he'd better sober up fast.

"Cass, do you have an aspirin?''

"In the medicine cabinet.''

"A compassionate woman would offer to get them.''

"If you can find one, suggest it. I'm busy. Some of us have to get to work this morning.''

"I'll get 'em myself.''

"Wise man.''

J.K. got the aspirin, took three and sat back down, praying that Cassie wouldn't get it into her head to start singing until they took effect. He sipped his coffee and pondered her attitude toward Ryan. She had sounded pretty sure of herself and he'd always credited her with knowing her own mind.

He looked up at her and announced casually, "He wants you back, you know."

"No, he doesn't," she replied just as casually.

"Cassie, I saw the way the man looked at you. I, of all people, can recognize lust when I see it."

"Then you also know that there's a rather wide gap between lust and love. Ryan just had a momentary twinge of jealousy. He picked up on the vibes between you and me and decided to get all territorial."

"He made a pass before I ever showed up," J.K. reminded her.

"Doesn't matter. Whatever the timing, he wasn't serious about it. It's instinct with him. I'm woman. He's man. Let's go for it. That's how he operates."

"Did you?"

"Did I what?"

"Go for it?"

"You seem to be missing the point here. I am not interested in my ex-husband, thank you very much. As for him, I guarantee he'll forget all about me the instant some sweet young thing winks at him from the bleachers." She put a plate of eggs, bacon and pancakes in front of him. "You know I'm right, so I'll ask you again, why'd you get so worked up over it?"

"I just didn't want to see you get hurt again," J.K. said, poking a fork tentatively into the center of the egg. The sight of all that yellow oozing out almost did him in. He covered it quickly with a pancake, then looked up just in time to see Cassie trying to wipe a smile off her too-expressive face. She seemed to know

something he didn't or at least she thought she did. He
couldn't imagine what.

"I don't think so," she responded, blithely digging
into her own breakfast. She was apparently having no
problems at all with her appetite.

J.K. was too busy trying to follow the conversation
to eat. Still baffled by her attitude, he said, "You think
I want to see you get hurt?"

"Of course not. I just don't think that's the whole
story and until you can figure out the rest, maybe
you'd better not come around so much."

He stared at her blankly. "Now why would you say
a fool thing like that? I thought you and I were working on a real relationship."

"I thought so, too."

"Then what's the problem?"

"I don't have one. You're the one who's drinking
and behaving like an adolescent."

"One little attack of jealousy," he grumbled. "You
go and make a big deal out of it."

"Unjustified jealousy," she noted. "And all I'm
suggesting is that you figure out why you found it so
tough to think of me out with Ryan."

"Because..." He couldn't think of a reason that
made a bit of sense.

"Because why?"

"Damn, woman! I never thought I'd say this, but
you're a hard woman, Cassie," he said, scowling at
her. "I'm hurting here and you're playing word games
with me."

She shrugged indifferently, changing forever his
image of her as sweet and vulnerable. Cassie was

tough as nails. Her words confirmed it. "Maybe so," she said as if she rather enjoyed the idea of giving him grief. "I just know what I see." That secretive look was back on her face.

"Which is?"

"I'm not going to be the one to say it, J.K."

"Cassie!"

"Eat your breakfast."

They ate in stubborn silence, J.K. trying to figure out what bee Cassie had in her bonnet now. He'd be damned if he could understand a woman who got such a kick out of talking in riddles.

"I guess I'll be going," he said eventually, expecting an argument or at least a mild protest.

"I hope you feel better," she said just as nonchalantly. "Though you don't deserve to."

He glared at her. "I'll just say goodbye to Teddy."

"Fine."

He walked into the family room still muttering under his breath. Cassie was singing happily before he reached the door, the off-key tune grating on his nerves worse than squeaking chalk on a blackboard. What did she have to be so blasted cheerful about? Since he wasn't likely to come up with an answer to that one, he turned his attention to Teddy, who was lying on the floor in front of the TV on his stomach, his chin propped in his hands. He barely spared a glance for J.K. Apparently the whole damn family was uninterested in his presence this morning.

"So, what're you watching?" J.K. asked after staring at the dizzying rush of colorful cartoon action for several minutes.

"It's about these giant bugs," Teddy explained enthusiastically. "They turn into people sometimes and nobody knows that they're really bad guys until it's too late and they zap 'em with these poison things."

J.K. nodded. The explanation made about as much sense as his conversation with Cassie.

"Wanna watch with me?" Teddy asked hopefully.

"Maybe for a minute," J.K. agreed, sitting down on the floor. Teddy promptly snuggled closer.

"See," he said, pointing. "That's one of the bad guys. Any minute now he's gonna kill the good guy, unless this guy Lionel can get there in time to save him."

"Lionel?" Whatever happened to the really tough guys like the Duke or Rambo, J.K. wondered, feeling increasingly out of sorts.

"Yeah, Lionel's really neat. He's in comic books and everything." Teddy paused. "Can I ask you something, Uncle Jake?"

"You can ask me anything."

"What's love?"

Oh, brother. It was not a question to ask a man with a boot-stomping jamboree going on in his head. "Ask me an easy one, pal."

"Don't you know?" Teddy asked, obviously surprised by this gap in his knowledge.

"I'm not sure I do," he said frankly. "What does you mom say?"

"She says there are different kinds of love. She says my dad can still love me, even if he doesn't love her anymore. Do you think that's right?"

J.K. felt the weight of all sorts of childish terrors behind that question. Teddy's expression was serious as he waited for an answer. "Absolutely," J.K. told him. "I think your dad loves you very much."

"I wish he'd come to see me more," he said wistfully. "It's great having a dad who's on television sometimes and stuff, but I miss having him around to, you know, hang out with. It was really neat seeing him yesterday, don't you think? Why do you think he and my mom don't live together anymore?"

"Grown-ups can't always get along the way they should when they're married. When that happens, sometimes it's better if they don't stay married anymore."

"You don't have a wife. Is that why? 'Cause you didn't get along?"

"Nope. You know I've never been married."

Suddenly Teddy's eyes lit up with excitement and he sat up. He put his hands on J.K.'s knees and leaned in close. "I know what, Uncle Jake."

"What?" J.K. said cautiously.

"You and Mom could get married!" he announced, clearly thrilled with the cleverness of his idea. "Wouldn't that be great? Then you'd be my dad, too. I'd have two dads."

Maybe if he'd been anticipating it, J.K. wouldn't have been so stunned. Instead, he reacted as if Teddy had suggested that he fly to the moon. Married? To Cassie? He wasn't sure which idea startled him more. He supposed that in the back of his mind he'd envisioned getting married one of these days, maybe after he'd left baseball behind him. But now? To Cassie?

"I don't think so," he protested, too quickly. Disappointment registered immediately on Teddy's face. He immediately felt guilt welling up. "Sorry, sport."

Teddy's excited expression began to change. He looked more indignant, though, than hurt. "How come? You like her, don't you? You come over a lot. That must mean you like her some."

"Of course I like her."

"Well, then?" His voice faltered. "Is it me, Uncle Jake? I'd be really good. I wouldn't be any trouble at all."

Oh, hell. "Teddy, this has nothing to do with you. You're the greatest kid in the whole world and I'd love to have you for my son. It's just..." He felt himself floundering.

"It's that love stuff, isn't it?" Teddy said wisely. "You don't love her?"

"Yeah, it's that love stuff," he agreed softly, but as Teddy turned back to the TV, J.K. began to wonder.

What if... The images that swept through his mind were powerful and seductive. Cassie had everything he'd ever wanted in a woman, at least those qualities that he'd ticked off on the rare occasions when he'd taken a serious look at the future. She was bright and beautiful and stubborn as the dickens. She'd never be dull. And loving. God, how he'd envied Ryan the tenderness in Cassie's eyes when she'd looked up at him on the day that Teddy had been born. Someday, he'd said to himself then. Someday, he'd have a woman like that. A woman who wasn't a bit like his cheating mother.

Well, why not now? And why not Cassie?

Because she wouldn't have him on a bet. It was as simple as that. Cassie was looking for reliability, steadfastness of heart and sensitivity. She credited him with none of those qualities. Even though he'd been on his best behavior for weeks now, she still didn't trust him worth spit. She tended to regard him with a prejudiced eye.

And rightly so, he admitted guiltily. He'd seduced her the first chance he got and hadn't said the first thing about the future.

That didn't mean he wasn't capable of changing, though. He'd win her over. She was already attracted to him. That was definitely no problem. He'd just have to prove to her that he was also the most reliable, the most faithful, the most sensitive man she'd ever met. Now that a plan was beginning to crystallize in his mind, J.K. could hardly wait to get started.

There was only one tiny little problem. How did he go about proving all that to a woman who already knew him better than he knew himself?

Eleven

———

J.K. had pitched no-hit ball games that were less stressful than planning this campaign of his to get Cassie to take him seriously. It took him a full week to figure out his first tactic, an endless week during which he denied himself the pleasure of even calling her, a week during which he growled at everyone else. His teammates began to give him a wide berth. Maria, however, had no such instinct for self-preservation.

"You are a fool if you do not see what is before your very eyes, J.K. Starr," she told him, her own eyes flashing.

"What are you talking about?"

"Cassie. She is in love with you."

"No, she's not."

Maria acted as if he hadn't spoken. "And you, I think, are in love with her, *si?*"

His gaze narrowed. "What makes you think that?"

"You have all the, how do you say, evidence."

"Symptoms," he corrected automatically, then looked at her. "It's that obvious?"

"It is to me. I see the way your eyes follow her. It is definitely the look of love. My Davey look at me that way before I get so huge," she said, rubbing her pregnant belly.

J.K. detected a certain wistfulness in her voice, something he probably would never have noticed if he weren't so attuned to shifts of mood these days. He hugged her. "Davey will always look at you that way."

Maria beamed. "You think so?"

"I know so."

"You see, that is why Cassie is in love with you. You have the charm, the gift of words."

"I'm not sure she sees that as an attribute," he admitted candidly.

Maria's expression grew puzzled. "What is this—attribute?"

"It means she doesn't take my charm all that seriously. She thinks it's a flaw."

"Cassie may see you with wide-open eyes, but that is good, is it not? She will never expect what you cannot give."

"Oh, I think she expects quite a lot and she deserves it."

"But not more than you can give," Maria insisted. "Have you told her how you felt?"

"Not yet."

"Why not? It does no good to speak to me of your feelings. Cassie is the one who needs to hear."

"It's going to take more than words."

"Then show her."

He grinned. "You make it sound so easy, Maria."

"It should be easy to speak what is in your heart."

But it wasn't. For the first time in his life, J.K.'s glib charm and clever seductiveness let him down. He sent flowers. He called. He thought of a dozen different ways to surprise her. She responded exactly the way he'd hoped, with enthusiasm and delight. But there was always a sense of reserve. It was as if she was still waiting for something else. He was damned if he could figure out how many other ways there were to say he loved her. The longer the emotional limbo went on, the more frayed his nerves became. While one part of him wondered if they would ever work things out, another part, a part he didn't acknowledge except in the darkest hours of the night, was terrified that they would.

Cassie decided she had a surprisingly sadistic streak. She was really enjoying watching J.K. squirm. Now that she'd recognized exactly how deep his feelings for her were and accepted that her own feelings ran just as deep, she could sit back and watch the developments with a certain amount of equanimity.

It was interesting, she decided from a purely objective, psychological standpoint, that the number of bouquets arriving decreased in direct proportion to the increasing seriousness of J.K.'s intentions. And without the tulips and daffodils and irises to boost his cause, J.K. seemed to be floundering. She considered it a good omen that he'd apparently never reached this stage with another relationship. She also knew that he had to face this part of the struggle on his own. He had to believe in the power of their love or it would never work. He thought he had only to overcome her doubts. She realized he had to overcome his own.

It was after midnight when the phone beside her bed rang. Predictably. J.K. apparently saw these late-night calls as a way of offering proof that she was always on his mind. She wondered if he also saw that he was testing her, checking on her, still doubting after all this time that any woman would remain faithful for long. Either way, if he didn't realize soon that what they had was built on mutual trust, she was going to be walking around like a sleep-starved zombie.

"Hi, J.K.," she murmured into the receiver, a smile in her voice.

"How'd you know it was me?"

"Who else would be calling at this hour? Where are you?"

"Tampa. In my motel room," he added hurriedly. "Alone."

Clearly he wanted to cover all the bases, relieve all her doubts.

"J.K., it's not that I don't appreciate these reports. I do. It's just that you seem to have a slightly misguided reason for giving them."

"I just want you to know that you're the only woman I care about. I thought if I called you'd begin to understand how I feel."

"I do understand, but the calls aren't the reason it's so clear."

"They're not?"

"Sweetheart, for all I know you could engage in wild revelry the minute you hang up. You could have women locked in your bathroom, even as we speak. You could leave the room and head to the nearest bar and drink till dawn. I'd never know it unless Davey or Kyle tattled and we all know how likely that is to happen."

"Oh," he said, sounding deflated. "I never thought of that. Should I call back later? Check in more often? Do you want to call me?"

She laughed. "Oh, J.K., don't you see? It's all a matter of trust. If I didn't trust you, you could call me every hour on the hour and it wouldn't matter. The reverse is just as true. Do you worry about what I'm doing while you're out of town?"

"Of course not."

"Why?"

"Because I trust you implicitly. You'd never cheat on me."

"You thought I might with Ryan."

"Just a temporary aberration." There was a long silence. "Wasn't it?"

"It was," she assured him.

"So, you're telling me I'm wasting my time making these calls."

"Not if all you want is a chance to say good-night." She lowered her voice seductively. "I very much like hearing your voice just before I go to sleep."

There was a heavy sigh on the other end of the line. "I miss you, Cass."

"I miss you, too."

"Good night, my love."

"Night, J.K."

When J.K. hung up the phone, he took yet another cold shower, then climbed into the too-empty king-size bed. He plumped up the pillows just right. He fussed with the sheets until they were just so over his naked body. He turned out the light. And his brain promptly went into overdrive with thoughts of Cassie. Sweet, sensual, arousing thoughts. Thoughts that sent him straight back into an icy shower.

Maybe it was time to stop all these subtle approaches, which didn't seem to be working anyway, and just tell her straight out what was on his mind. Maybe that's what Maria had been suggesting days ago. He could handle rejection. Probably. He wasn't so sure he could deal with having her laugh in his face, but Cassie would never do anything quite that tacky. Probably.

Thank heavens they were going home after tomorrow's game. Maybe once he'd kissed her, maybe after he'd held her in his arms, he wouldn't feel this sense of urgency. Maybe he'd be able to hold off actually asking her to marry him until he was sure he'd convinced her how much he'd changed. With something this important, he wanted all the odds stacked in his favor.

So, he decided, back in bed again with the light out, he'd slow down, hold off until the timing was exactly right. It was the sensible way to go.

"Marry me, Cassie," he blurted out seconds after he'd walked into her living room. She wasn't even looking at him when he said it. She was down on her knees looking for dust or something. J.K. knew it was all wrong, but the words just popped out automatically. It probably had something to do with standing there while her cute little derriere was poked up at him. He waited, holding his breath, for her reaction.

She wasn't laughing. He could tell that. She also wasn't moving. Maybe she wasn't even breathing. She'd probably gone into shock.

"Cass?" He bent down beside her. "Did you hear me?"

She rocked back on her heels and stared into his eyes. "You're serious, aren't you?"

He didn't trust himself to repeat the words again. He just nodded, hoping she could tell exactly how much love there was in his heart.

"Why, J.K.? Why now?"

"Because... Why does anyone ask somebody to get married? You know..."

"I can think of any number of reasons to get married. People marry for money. They marry for position. They marry out of some sense of family obligation. They get married because they can't stay out of bed and figure they ought to legalize it. So, J.K., which is it in your case?"

He could think of only one way to shut her up, to halt all this ridiculous talk of arranged marriages and get-rich-quick marriages. He kissed her. Long and slow and hard, until they were both so breathless neither of them could speak.

Cassie swallowed hard, her eyes dazed. "That's definitely one reason," she said, her voice a husky whisper.

"A good one?"

"Not bad."

"Not bad? Obviously I didn't do my best. Let's try again," he said, claiming her lips with every bit of mastery at his command.

"Oh, my," she said weakly.

He regarded her indignantly. "Is *oh, my* better than *not bad?*"

There was just the tiniest bit of amusement in her eyes. "About the same," she said, being deliberately provoking. Maybe this marriage idea he'd had was lousy, after all. Did he want to spend the rest of his life with a woman who taunted him?

Damn right he did.

"Do you want to be swept off your feet, carried off to bed and loved for forty-eight hours straight?" he asked, searching for a more successful approach.

She grinned at that. "You're definitely getting warmer."

"Damn right I am," he growled. "I'm burning up and so are you. What are we talking about here? You need a grand seduction to convince you?"

She sighed and shook her head. "Nope. I like the concept, but it's not the answer."

J.K. got to his feet and began to pace. "I don't get it. I've done everything I can think of. Are you just not in love with me? Is that it? Maria thinks you are, but maybe she's got it all wrong, too. Does she?"

She halted him in midstep by grabbing his hand and kissing his knuckles. Her velvet lips caressing his scarred flesh sent bolts of lightning flashing through him. "Cass?"

"You're off base, J.K. I do love you. I do trust you. I began to trust you weeks ago, when you ignored every bitchy, obnoxious thing I said and did and just kept trying to help. I think I fell in love with you when you were dumping peanut butter and grape jelly into my grocery cart. I saw exactly how caring, how sweet you were capable of being."

"You love me?" he repeated, dazed. He lifted her up until she was standing, then studied her. "Really? No doubts?"

"Not a one."

He dropped her hands and shoved his own hands through his hair. "Then I really don't get it. Why haven't you said yes?"

"Because I want to hear you say the words, J.K. I want you to admit that you love me. I know what you feel in your heart. I can tell it by the way you treat me, the way you treat Teddy. But I think it's important for you to recognize that it's really true."

"Why the hell else would I be asking you to marry me?"

She grinned, apparently taking great delight in his frustration. "Shall I run through the list again?"

"No. Forget it. Once was enough."

"Why can't you say the words, J.K.? Do you know the answer to that?"

He sank down on the sofa. He searched his brain and then his heart. He probably should have started with the latter. "I suppose it's because of what you said a few weeks ago," he admitted finally.

"About your mother?"

"Yes. I guess so. Ever since I found out what she was really like, I've never believed a woman could make an honest commitment."

"Yet you seem to think that I can."

"You're different, Cass."

She shook her head. "Am I really so different, J.K., or are you finally realizing that you've been intentionally setting out to fulfill your own expectations?"

He twisted her explanation around, stood it on end and still didn't know what the hell she was talking about. "Cassie, I'm not here for some psychobabble stuff. Talk English or we can forget the whole thing."

"Just think for a minute, J.K. You've always chosen exactly the kind of woman you knew would let you down. Then you dumped them, before they could move on leaving you behind."

There was something undeniably familiar about the pattern she described. "That's sick."

"Not so sick," she said. "A fairly normal reaction to the hurt you felt when you found out about your mother. But if we're going to make this work, J.K., it's every bit as important for you to trust me as it is for me to trust you. If you've just decided to marry me because it's time to settle down, we'll never make it."

"That's not it, Cass. I swear it. I love you."

"Well, hallelujah! Finally."

He grinned at her exuberance. "Okay, so it took me a long time to wake up to that. There might even have been a time when I figured if you were attracted to me, but still in love with Ryan, it made you like all the others...." He stopped, suddenly realizing what he'd said.

Cassie nodded as if she'd guessed it all along.

"That's why I went so crazy thinking you were going back to Ryan, isn't it? I thought you were just another cheating wife and it was tearing me apart inside."

All at once he felt totally drained. Tapping into the depths of his emotions was harder than anything he'd ever done before. It was worth it, though, if it meant he and Cassie were going to get off to the right start.

"I love you, Cass," he said again, this time with full understanding of the words. "Marry me."

Cassie's eyes were shining and even before she spoke he could read the answer in her joyous expression. "Yes, J.K. Yes!" she said, her fingers tunneling into his hair as she drew his head down for a kiss.

When he could finally draw a steady breath again, J.K. asked, "Is Teddy home?"

"Nope."

"Is he likely to come home in the next half hour?"

"Half hour?" she repeated with exaggerated disappointment.

"Okay," he said, grinning. "Make it an hour. Are we going to be alone for at least an hour?"

"I think we can count on that. Why?"

"Because I have plans for you, Cassie Miles. I've been thinking about these plans every night for the last week. I've almost gone crazy thinking about them."

"Sounds intriguing."

"That's one word for them," J.K. said wryly. "Let me show you."

He lifted her into his arms and carried her down the hall. "First the shower," he said. "Do you have any idea how much time I've spent in showers this past week?"

"Are you so sure talking me into this one with you will be the solution to this problem you seem to have?"

"It will definitely be a solution to my most immediate problem. If you're concerned about the memories it's likely to arouse, I'll take my chances."

He flipped on the water, then slowly removed Cassie's clothes. His followed in quick succession. He drew her into the shower stall and picked up a bar of soap as the water cascaded around them. His hands slippery and sudsy, he began to wash her, his gaze riveted on the changes in her body as his touches became bolder and bolder. His fingers skimmed and teased, sliding over slick flesh until he could bear it no more. He lifted her slightly, settling her on him, his blood roaring, his body demanding. Her legs wrapped tight around his waist and her breasts were crushed against his chest. Only the slowest, most tantalizing movement was possible.

"Cassie," he whispered, his voice a tender moan. "God, how I've dreamed of this. Night after night. I haven't been able to get the feel of you out of my head."

The water turned to steam as their body temperature soared. "It's like the movie," she said, wonder in her voice and dazed sensuality in her eyes.

"But we're real, sweetheart. This is real."

Her head fell back and he pressed his lips against the hollow at her throat. "Sweet, sweet Cassie. I've been so hungry for you." He tasted fiery shoulders and slickened breasts as the slow rocking motion began to send gentle waves washing through him. The tempo of the waves increased, more demanding, crashing endlessly until at last they both shouted out with the sheer ecstasy of it.

J.K. reached behind him and turned off the water. When his legs were steady again, he wrapped Cassie in a towel and carried her to bed. "I never want to sleep another night without you beside me," he said, wiping strands of damp, blond hair from her cheeks.

"Not very realistic, all things considered," she said with a sigh that seemed heavy with regret.

"Cass, that is something we have to talk about."

"I don't want to talk, J.K."

"But we have to. Are you going to be okay about my playing baseball and being on the road so much? You brought up the subject of trust and I know right now you're convinced I'm being honest and honorable, but how long is it likely to be before the doubts set in?"

She tried to roll away from him, but he held her tight. "Come on, babe. Be honest."

"I can't answer that. I guess it depends on you."

"How so?""

"J.K., when I married Ryan he was already playing baseball. I knew what the life would be like or at least I had a pretty good idea. I didn't go nuts just because we were separated a lot. It all changed when I found out he was cheating on me. That's what ruined the relationship. The discovery that I couldn't trust him anymore."

"So you'll trust me until I let you down?"

"I guess that's about the size of it."

He leaned back, bringing her with him. Her head was resting on his chest. "I wish I could believe that."

"It's true. You're not the same man Ryan is."

"You haven't always felt that way."

"You've won me over," she said lightly.

"At the risk of indulging in some of that psycho-babble I accused you of earlier, I think your vision may be clouded by your hormones. The reality is that you've been hurt by a man very much like me, who used his road travel as an excuse to be unfaithful. I don't want you getting nervous every time I pack my bags. Be honest, Cassie. There's a part of you that's going to be threatened."

"Maybe so," she admitted finally, angrily. "But I'll deal with it."

"There has to be a better way."

"Name one."

"You and Teddy will just have to come with me," he said at once, liking the prospect. "I'm not a bit crazier about the idea of leaving you behind than you are about being left."

"Not very practical."

"I'm not looking for practical. I'm looking for a way we can guarantee that this marriage will work."

"There are no guarantees, J.K."

"Maybe not, but we can sure as hell improve the odds. We'll just have to make the travel thing work."

"That's all well and good during the summer, but Teddy has school and I have work."

"You won't need to work."

"But I'm not so sure I want to become totally dependent on you or any man."

"Sweetheart, if you want a career I'm all for it, but couldn't it wait until I retire in a few years and we can settle down in one place? Maybe you could just take classes during the off-season and get that degree you were talking about. Then you'd be ready for a really good job."

"I suppose I could do that. But what about Teddy's school?"

As hard as he tried, J.K. couldn't come up with an answer to that one. "I guess that gives us about four months of the year—April and May, maybe a little of June, then September and part of October—when we're going to be separated, at least some of the time."

"Unless," Cassie began slowly. "J.K., what if we moved up north? You'd only be down here for the few weeks of spring training. The rest of the time you'd be home, except for road trips and we could at least come along on weekends."

He let the suggestion settle in his mind. It definitely had some merit. "I suppose that's workable," he said. "You really want to leave here?"

"I told you how much I've been missing snow and the change of seasons. I wouldn't want to go back forever, I don't think, but for a few years I think it would be great. What do you think?"

"I think you're a pretty terrific lady."

"You're pretty wonderful yourself."

"So, Cassie Miles, do you think we can make this marriage thing work?"

She scattered little kisses all over his chest.

"Is that your answer?" he inquired, his pulse quickening.

"Yes," she whispered. "My final answer. I wonder what Teddy's going to think of all this?"

"He'll love it," J.K. said confidently.

"You sound so sure of that."

"I am. It was his idea."

"What?"

"It might have been a little unorthodox, but your son proposed to me weeks ago, on your behalf of course."

"You're kidding."

"Nope. Obviously that's one very bright child. He recognized what we hadn't figured out yet."

"Remind me to raise his allowance," she said. She was still in his embrace for the longest time before she added, "Thank you, J.K."

"For what?" he said.

"For loving me."

"It seems as natural as breathing," he said, realizing it was true.

"Do you know how rare it is, though, to find what we've found?" she demanded, then grinned. "Besides, how many women can claim they have their very own Midnight Starr to light up the night?"

"Oh, Cassie," he said, laughing. "We are going to have one helluva good time together, aren't we?"

She snuggled closer. "The very best," she said softly. "The very best."

* * * * *

BEGINNING IN FEBRUARY FROM

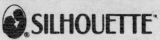

SILHOUETTE

Western Lovers

An exciting new series by Elizabeth Lowell
Three fabulous love stories
Three sexy, tough, tantalizing heroes

In February, *Man of the Month* Tennessee Blackthorne in
OUTLAW
In March, Cash McQueen in *GRANITE MAN*
In April, Nevada Blackthorne in *WARRIOR*

WESTERN LOVERS—Men as tough and untamed as
the land they call home.

Only in *Silhouette Desire*!

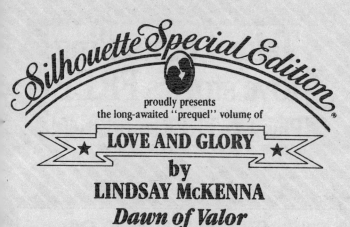

Silhouette Special Edition

proudly presents
the long-awaited "prequel" volume of

★ LOVE AND GLORY ★

by
LINDSAY McKENNA
Dawn of Valor

In the summer of '89, Silhouette Special Edition premiered three novels celebrating America's men and women in uniform: LOVE AND GLORY, by bestselling author Lindsay McKenna. Featured were the proud Trayherns, a military family as bold and patriotic as the American flag—three siblings valiantly battling the threat of dishonor, determined to triumph . . . in love and glory.

Now, discover the roots of the Trayhern brand of courage, as parents Chase and Rachel relive their earliest heartstopping experiences of survival and indomitable love, in

Dawn of Valor, Silhouette Special Edition #649

This month, experience the thrill of LOVE AND GLORY—from the very beginning!

Available at your favorite retail outlet, or order your copy by sending your name, address, zip or postal code, along with a check or money order (please do not send cash) for $2.95, plus 75¢ postage and handling, payable to Silhouette Reader Service to:

In the U.S.
3010 Walden Ave
P.O. Box 1396
Buffalo, NY 14269- 396

In Canada
P.O. Box 609
Fort Erie, Ontario
L2A 5X3

Please specify book title with your order. Canadian residents add applicable federal and provincial taxes.

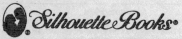

Silhouette Books®

DV-1A

Take 4 bestselling love stories FREE

Plus get a FREE surprise gift!

Special Limited-time Offer

Silhouette Reader Service®

Mail to

In the U.S.	In Canada
3010 Walden Avenue	P.O. Box 609
P.O. Box 1867	Fort Erie, Ontario
Buffalo, N.Y. 14269-1867	L2A 5X3

YES! Please send me 4 free Silhouette Desire® novels and my free surprise gift. Then send me 6 brand-new novels every month, which I will receive months before they appear in bookstores. Bill me at the low price of $2.24* each—a savings of 26¢ apiece off cover prices. There are no shipping, handling or other hidden costs. I understand that accepting the books and gift places me under no obligation ever to buy any books. I can always return a shipment and cancel at any time. Even if I never buy another book from Silhouette, the 4 free books and the surprise gift are mine to keep forever.

*Offer slightly different in Canada—$2.24 per book plus 69¢ per shipment for delivery. Sales tax applicable in N.Y. Canadian residents add applicable federal and provincial sales tax.

225 BPA JAZP (US)   326 BPA 8177 (CAN)

Name	(PLEASE PRINT)	
Address		Apt. No.
City	State/Prov.	Zip/Postal Code

This offer is limited to one order per household and not valid to present Silhouette Desire® subscribers. Terms and prices are subject to change.

DES-BPADR   © 1990 Harlequin Enterprises Limited

SILHOUETTE·INTIMATE·MOMENTS®

WELCOME TO
FEBRUARY FROLICS!

This month, we've got a special treat in store for you: four terrific books written by four brand-new authors! From sunny California to North Dakota's frozen plains, they'll whisk you away to a world of romance and adventure.

Look for

L.A. HEAT (IM #369) by Rebecca Daniels
AN OFFICER AND A GENTLEMAN (IM #370) by Rachel Lee
HUNTER'S WAY (IM #371) by Justine Davis
DANGEROUS BARGAIN (IM #372) by Kathryn Stewart

They're all part of February Frolics, available now from Silhouette Intimate Moments—where life is exciting and dreams do come true.

FF-1A

SILHOUETTE·INTIMATE·MOMENTS®

NORA ROBERTS
Night Shadow

People all over the city of Urbana were asking, Who was that masked man?

Assistant district attorney Deborah O'Roarke was the first to learn his secret identity . . . and her life would never be the same.

The stories of the lives and loves of the O'Roarke sisters began in January 1991 with NIGHT SHIFT, Silhouette Intimate Moments #365. And if you want to know more about Deborah and the man behind the mask, look for NIGHT SHADOW, Silhouette Intimate Moments #373, available in March at your favorite retail outlet.

NITE-1

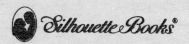

Silhouette Books®